D1564545

*There are none
so blind as those
who will not see.*

JONATHAN SWIFT

THE SOUND OF HONOR

*If your best friend's been murdered, even a
blind guy's got to take a shot in the dark ...*

BY JIM STOVALL

HAWK PUBLISHING : TULSA

HAWK Publishing Group
7107 South Yale, # 345
Tulsa OK 74136
www.hawkpub.com

Printed in the United States
COVER AND BOOK DESIGN: Carl Brune

ISBN 978-1-930709-70-6

HAWK and colophon are trademarks belonging to the HAWK Publishing Group.

DEDICATION

This book is dedicated to Bill Bernhardt and the people at Hawk Publishing who believed that a motivational business writer could become the author of a mystery.

It is also dedicated to Dorothy Thompson who, through twelve books, has turned my spoken words into print on the page.

And, finally, to the countless friends, relatives, and colleagues who help a blind guy like me live and succeed in the real world.

CHAPTER 1

There is a heavy mist that often drifts across the Arkansas River near downtown Tulsa, Oklahoma. This mist carries with it the distinct and unmistakable aroma of crude oil from the refineries on the west side of town. There has long been a debate among Tulsans as to whether this aroma is pleasant or disgusting. I have come to the conclusion that it is dependent upon whose oil one is smelling at any given point in time. I suspect the smell of one's own oil is much like the smell of the fine leather in a new sports car or Paris in springtime or the freshly-mown fairway at a world-class country club. I believe the smell of someone else's oil is much like desperation, greed, and envy. It puts one in mind of being on the outside, looking in.

I was experiencing the smell of oil and contemplating its meaning to me, or lack thereof, as I was skirting the edge of downtown, walking toward my office. It was very early in the morning, and the only sounds were a few trash trucks, air conditioners cycling off and on, and the sharp tapping of my cane on the sidewalk. My name is Jacob Dyer, Jake to my friends, and *that blind guy over there* to everyone else in the world who doesn't know me.

As I walked along the sidewalk, I was hearing, smelling, tasting, and feeling everything around me, letting my senses capture the morning. In reality, I was trying to occupy my mind and forget the urgent call I had received last night. "Jake, this is Rebecca—I mean Becky," she had said.

That brief introduction was sufficient in and of itself to propel me backward a thousand years into another life. I was instantly skimming the top of the jungle canopy in a helicopter somewhere in Southeast Asia. John Ivers, my best friend and pilot extraordinaire, was sitting on my left. As my body continued to automatically walk along the sidewalk, the past brutally invaded my mind. The colors flashed before me so vividly, I'm sure they have intensified over the years. I wasn't simply remembering it, I was there. That was all before the big explosion that made the world stand still and changed me into the Jake Dyer I have come to be in the last quarter century.

"I need to come and see you tomorrow morning, first thing. I need your help. I'm very scared, because I'm dealing with some dangerous people. I don't even have any money to pay you, but John always told me to remember that if everything ever fell apart and there was nowhere else to turn, call Jake."

I told her I would be happy to see her in the morning, and as I hung up, I said to myself, *Dyer, you only have three rules in the lost and found business. One: always get paid. Two: never get emotionally involved. Three: avoid dangerous people.* In one brief phone call, I had successfully shattered all three commandments I live by. I tried to shove the pending meeting and emotional ordeal from the forefront of my mind, realizing it would be more than I was able to handle.

It was going to be another hot day they had said on the radio during the 5 a.m. weather report. To call Oklahoma summers simply hot during the five months of suffering is to miss the adjectives ranging from miserable through oppressive.

As I rounded the corner onto 3rd Street, I heard the familiar voice of Leroy Small at the corner newsstand. "Another hot one, Jake," Leroy chanted. "Looks like the Arabs and the Jews are talking again, interest rates are stable, and some woman claims your president dropped his pants again." Leroy knows I can't read his newspapers, and he is convinced there is no other source of news in the world, so each morning he gives me his own, concise version of Leroy's News and Comment.

"It looks like my president may have better ongoing relations than the Jews and Arabs," I called to Leroy as I stepped into the revolving door of my office tower.

The Derrick Building is one of those marble and mahogany edifices that was built during the Depression when the oil flowed freely. Buildings like this are extravagant, impractical, and something I hold on to dearly as a relic representing a time gone by that we will never experience again. The lobby is two stories high and made of imported Italian marble. There is a spot in front of the far left elevator from which you can hear everything said on the entire first floor. This has come in handy for me more than once.

As I approached the far left elevator, the door slid open

as if on cue. I knew I was in for a great day. I pressed the button for the 14th floor, which for people like me who walk around in the dark is the seventh button on the right side. The elevator car rumbled and rattled up the shaft and groaned as it stopped on my floor. It's not like one of those modern, impersonal elevators that shoots you skyward without your even knowing. It's like an old friend with a few aches and pains, but you wouldn't have it any other way. I turned right as I exited the elevator and headed to the last door at the end of the hall. For those who are concerned about such things, the sign on the antique frosted glass says "Dyer Straits Lost and Found."

We are not investigators, not lawyers, and not anything else that's easy to describe. We simply stumble around and find things that people have lost when they have nowhere else to turn. At this point, I must say you would not be the first person, nor I'm sure the last, to think it strange that people retain a blind man for the express purpose of looking for something that they can't find. We have gotten used to this paradox in our professional lives.

The *we* I speak of is my assistant Monica and me. To describe Monica as an assistant is to describe the Grand Canyon as a slight depression. Monica is one of those rare people who can most accurately be described by simply saying, *They are the best at what they do.* She is the Michael Jordan, Mickey Mantle, and Muhammad Ali of our lost and found business. I have shared this with her in the past in an attempt to express my appreciation, but I fear the analogy is lost on her as I heard her once describe Ali as a large man who stands around in his underwear and hits people.

As I walked across our reception area which holds Monica's desk and everything she uses to make the world go 'round, I calculated I had a good four hours before she would make her daily grand entrance.

I folded up my collapsible white cane which, thankfully, is not necessary when I am in the familiar confines of my apartment or office. It is always a relief to get it folded up and put away, much like the relief I would feel if I removed a large sign hanging around my neck which described to everyone I pass throughout the day the most intense, painful, and private problems in my life. The cane and I have a perpetual love/hate relationship.

I opened the door to my office and crossed to my desk. I reached behind me and eased open the window. Another one of the numerous benefits of working in a dinosaur of a building is the fact that the windows really open, and you are not forced to breathe stale, used, recycled air all day. Monica has informed me in no uncertain terms that if we ever leave this building and move into one of those sealed-glass-test-tube-like office towers, that my beloved cigars will be permanently banned from the work environment. As this is such an inconceivable thought, I have resigned myself to the fact that I will either retire or die sitting in my corner office on the 14th floor of the Derrick Building.

I poured some spring water through the brass and aluminum monstrosity that is politely known as a designer coffee maker. I flipped the switch and contemplated the meaning of life as I waited for the life-sustaining caffeine concoction to present itself after being processed through my Aunt Mae's Christmas gift from last year. Once Aunt Mae saw the space-age, nuclear-powered coffee maker on the Home Shopping Network, my 17-year-old Mr. Coffee was forever doomed.

I leaned back in my decrepit leather chair that has warped

and sagged over the years. Fortunately, it has warped and sagged in the same places I have, so we get along just fine, thank you very much. As the futuristic coffee machine completed its ritual, I reached for my Donald Duck coffee cup and poured the first blessed cup of the day. I was pleased that I found Donald easily, and it appeared I had finally communicated to the Derrick Building's cleaning crew that I am blind, and the Donald Duck coffee cup is to remain in the same, exact location permanently—not close to the same location or about the same location—but exactly. If there's anything finer than the morning's first cup of double-strength coffee from Aunt Mae's 21st Century machine, I am not sophisticated enough to appreciate it.

To complete the morning ritual, I reached into the bottom, left drawer of my ancient mahogany desk. As files and paper of any type are a frustrating mystery to me and, therefore, not a part of my life, this file drawer space has been converted into what may be the world's first legal-sized file drawer humidor. I reached into the very back of the drawer where I have been hoarding some of the finest exports from the Dominican Republic. One can tell by simply holding this cigar that it was hand rolled by an artist of significant talent, wisdom, and grace. I clipped the end from this masterpiece, lit it with a solid gold Dunhill lighter which is a treasured gift from a friend beyond compare, and prepared to attack the day.

CHAPTER 2

s it was approaching 6 a.m., I got ready to make my first phone call of the day. Many people would think 6 a.m. is an inappropriate if not ungodly time to make a phone call. This sentiment would be further compounded if they considered I was preparing to call the West Coast where it was the enchanted hour of four in the morning. I pressed the memo button on our handy answering device and heard the incomparable voice of Miss Monica reading me the name and number of the subject of my first call of the day. I have often thought if there were a way to capture and bottle Monica's voice, we could get rich selling it by the six-pack and quit doing whatever it is we do here.

The purpose of my first call on this particular day was to locate someone who did not wish to be located. This can be a delicate and precarious task. But in our so-called civilized society, it is impossible to hide from someone who has patience, persistence, and a devious, warped mind.

Approximately one week earlier, I had been retained by the owner of a regional restaurant chain to find their accountant/ treasurer. I was informed that Leonard McGee had done a great job in accounting for all their money just before he took it all and disappeared. Through some round-about means, Monica and I had tracked him to a San Diego hotel room that he was purportedly sharing with an energetic young lady, thirty years his junior. We had discovered his trail via a cooperative young woman at the airlines ticket counter.

Monica and I have a policy in our lost and found business. We endeavor never to directly lie to anyone; however, if some people inadvertently get under the wrong impression, it is not our responsibility to correct them. The cooperative young ticket agent was very understanding when she was informed that the direct link to the modem back-up link to the modular hard drive had been experiencing some problems. She told me she fully understood this—which I found fascinating as I had just that moment made it up. She was more than willing to confirm that Mr. McGee had left Tulsa, and she provided flight numbers and the arrival time for his connection in Dallas and his final destination at San Diego Airport.

Monica's brilliance in allowing cab company dispatchers, hotel desk clerks, and security personnel to get under the wrong impression had yielded the name of Mr. McGee's hotel and his room number. Monica had already arranged to have one of our trusty West Coast contacts ensconced in the hotel lobby at 4 a.m. in readiness for the reaction to my phone call. Our West Coast contact had been instructed to tail Mr. McGee and keep us informed as to his whereabouts until our client could do whatever it was he chose to do with Mr. McGee.

Dyer Straits Lost and Found simply attempts to find whatever has been lost. The recovery, prosecution, or whatever our client desires, is left solely to the discretion of our clients whenever possible. People who have attempted to disappear and then are forced into the light of day are often unkind, impolite, and violent—just the kind of people you do not want to encounter any more than you have to—although I must admit over the years, I have had my share of close calls with the inevitable targets of our successful work.

As I dialed the phone, I remembered Monica's warning about calling a middle-aged accountant at four in the morning who has spent several days in the company of a college co-ed. She warned that if his heart gives out, so does our fee. Nevertheless, I asked a very sleepy-sounding night clerk to put the call through to room 608. He asked me if I had any idea what time it was. I told him that it was 4:07 in the morning according to my watch and this was a medical emergency. I explained to him that if a spleen is harvested and not transplanted within two hours, the results are most always fatal. He seemed to gather the right amount of concern and urgency in his voice as he put the call through. He said, "Thank you, sir, and God bless you."

As the phone began ringing in 608, I imagined the accountant and the co-ed being abruptly awakened from a deep slumber. On the fourth ring, the phone was obviously knocked to the floor and a semi-comatose co-ed said, "Yeah."

I immediately intoned, "Young lady, this is a Dyer medical emergency. I need to speak to Mr. McGee immediately."

After an extremely long pause, with a hand held over the

phone and some conversation in the background, she came back on to tell me that Mr. McGee was not there. I explained to her the frailty of the human spleen and the fact that a patient's very life was in her capable hands. After another long pause and muffled conversation, I heard the voice that I assumed to be Leonard McGee. "Who is this?" he asked.

As I mentally patted myself on the back for another impossible job well done, I declared, "Mr. McGee, my name is Jacob Dyer, and in the grand scheme of things, in the veritable giant game of tag we all play as an integral part of our daily lives, you, my dear sir, are now officially *It*. You can run, but can't hide."

The receiver was immediately slammed down on the other end of the line, and I chuckled as I visualized Mr. McGee trying to locate his briefcase full of stolen money, his car keys, and his pants as he tried to explain to a junior college history major that *A spleen has nothing to do with it. Just shut up!*

I put on a Mozart CD and began dictating the detailed and extensive report we would submit to our client recounting our heroic deeds justifying the sizable bill. I knew that the Mozart music in the background of my dictation would be a subtle touch to be fully appreciated by magnificent Monica.

I was tapping the last ash from my Dominican work of art when our West Coast operative called letting me know that Mr. McGee had seen the error of his ways and had been tailed to a local police station. I let our West Coast man know he had done a stellar job and told him to have a cold one on me. He grumbled as he let me know that it was not quite yet seven in the morning in California, and he signed off utilizing a phrase that I do not find acceptable for inclusion within these chronicles.

I called our client, letting him know of our success, as well as how and where he could get in touch with Mr. McGee and his ill-gotten gains. Our client was emotional, thankful, and let me know how brilliant he thought I was. I agreed with him and let him know that our bill would be forthcoming and would reflect my brilliance.

As I hung up the phone and placed the dictation cassette with the Mozart mood music in my out basket, I heard the bell at the outer door ring, letting me and everyone on the 14th floor know that her highness, the grand princess, Miss Monica was making her morning entrance.

## CHAPTER 3

Monica Stone is a product of the Creator that defies description. The best I can do is to simply say that Monica is the essence of life. When she enters, everything seems to be electrically charged.

As a blind person, I have discovered that I can sense the location of things and particularly people I can't see. Some people have to get within a few feet before I can tell they have arrived, but if Monica is anywhere in the general vicinity, every fiber of my being is aware of it instantly. I know that she is a gorgeous creature, because I have been with her in public. She can walk into a crowded room, and everyone instantly freezes, sort of like the old E. F. Hutton commercial. She has single-handedly caused many traffic tie-ups and several actual accidents outside our office building.

Leroy has told me that his day officially begins when he watches Monica walk by. Leroy is convinced that all that beauty is wasted on a blind man. I have assured him that it is not, because in my own way, even though I have never seen her, I know that she is incomparably beautiful. Monica's moods range from extreme highs to somewhere in orbit with very little in between, and these moods can change faster than stormy weather during an Oklahoma spring.

On that particular morning, I remember Monica breezing into the office, calling, "Good morning, Jake. Do you want a bagel? I brought you a cinnamon raisin with light cream cheese. I know you like those best, and I told the man you didn't want any of his coffee because you said it was like swamp water. They took forever to get the bagels, and they almost dropped them off the counter. I nearly broke a nail!"

Monica can carry on an entire conversation by herself. If at any point in time I choose not to participate, I know she can pick up the slack. I was very grateful that she had not broken a nail, because this can start a tail spin of events that can end the entire day with a massive crash and burn.

I told Monica that I had successfully closed the file on the Leonard McGee disappearance. She simply mumbled, "Great," and launched into a monologue recounting the benefits of light cream cheese.

When she first came into my life, I was offended when she did not pay enough attention to my successes to feed my sizable ego. In more recent years, I have come to realize that the greatest compliment one can ever receive is the one that Monica pays me regularly as she simply expects success and is in no way surprised when everything comes together as planned.

I have now lived over half of my life as a blind person. I

know the frustration and degradation one can feel when no one expects me to be able to perform the most simple and mundane daily tasks on my own. Sometimes my greatest desire is to just be normal. Monica does not simply treat me normally; she holds me to a higher standard of performance, and this is one of the myriad things I love about her.

I handed her the dictation cassette and told her that it contained my report of the case we had just closed, and I asked if she could get it typed up and send it along with an appropriate bill to our grateful client.

She left my bagel in the pre-agreed, officially-designated bagel spot at a 45 degree angle from Donald's beak. She headed toward the outer office, but stopped in the doorway and turned to inquire, "Do I get any mood music this morning?"

I explained that she would be typing to the angelic strains of Wolfgang Amadeus Mozart today as a recorded background to my dictated report.

"You gotta love it," she said as she began her morning routine.

Realizing that Donald Duck was nearly depleted, I poured my second cup of the day, leaned back in my chair, and listened to the city noises filtering in through the open window.

As I cleared my mind of the previous case, I couldn't help but think about Becky Ivers' call last night and realized that she would be in shortly.

There are certain people, sounds, and smells that immediately transport us to another time and another place. My fourth grade teacher, Mrs. Livingston, still lives here in Tulsa, and I run into her from time to time when I am on my ritual walks to and from the office. Mrs. Livingston must be 80 years old now, and I am on the rusty side of 40, but all she need do is say, "Good morning, Jacob," and I am instantly 9 years old and grasping for an excuse as to why my math homework was not completed.

Of all the things in my world that can trigger a memory, nothing is more powerful than the image of the time and place I shared with John Ivers. The mere sound of his wife Becky's voice took me back to a war that was too complex to understand, especially for a 19-year-old Okie. Now that I consider myself a worldly, debonair, educated intellectual of 40-something, I understand less about Vietnam than I did then.

# # #

I first met John Ivers on an Army transport bus the initial day of basic training. A number of raw recruits, including myself, had been dropped off on a concrete parking lot outside the barbed wire gate of the base. We were told by a gentleman of limited vocabulary, but impressive volume, to *Stand right there, and do not move!* I was later to discover that the Army is full of people who make up for lack of vocabulary with volume.

Eventually, the bus arrived to take us somewhere. As it pulled up in front of us, another gentleman endowed with great volume stood on the bottom step of the bus and yelled at us, questioning our lack of intelligence and dubious family lineage. He then told us to form up and get on the bus. As I wasn't sure quite what that meant, I followed everyone else in line.

This gentleman, who I later learned would be our drill instructor for the next several months that seemed like an eternity, continued yelling at us as he tried to step backwards onto the next highest step of the bus. He slipped and took a comical fall directly onto his blessed assurance. Everyone else was frozen with fear, but I was so nervous, the only thing I could do was laugh out loud.

When the sergeant finally collected himself, stood up, and bounded down the stairs of the bus to the parking lot, I discovered that his heretofore extreme volume was only the beginning of his vocal capacity. He walked up and down the line of us, screaming the question, "Who laughed?"

Without hesitation, John stepped forward with a smirk on his face that I came to love in years to come, and said, "I did, sir."

Over the next several weeks, I have no idea how many push-ups John did, how many laps he ran, or potatoes he peeled. The sergeant went out of his way for our entire time in basic training to make life miserable for all of us and a living Hell for John.

That first night in the barracks as we dragged ourselves into our bunks, I asked John why he had done that. He smirked and said, "Sometimes, Okie, you just gotta do the right thing. Maybe someday you can do something for me."

#. #. #.

That episode and hundreds of others flooded my mind as I remembered the person I used to be in a time and place so far removed from my 14th floor corner office in my beloved Derrick Building.

Just then, Monica tapped on my door, opened it, stepped inside my office, and eased the door closed behind her. She let me know that Rebecca Ivers had arrived for her scheduled appointment and was nervously waiting in the outer office.

Monica then did one of the things that she does so very well. She used that photographic mind of hers to give me a verbal image of the woman waiting to meet me. Monica can do this for a person, a place, or a thing and somehow has the capacity to tell me exactly what I need to know without any emotion, unnecessary detail, and without robbing me of the dignity I need to do my job.

Monica sat down and told me, "She looks like she's late 40s or early 50s, but I don't think this is one of her better days. I don't think she's had better days in a long time. She's actually probably closer to forty-two or -three. Her best efforts at makeup are pretty good, but they don't disguise the fact that she hasn't slept well in a long time. Her dress is conservative, moderate price mall department store. Her shoes are sensible, and she has no outstanding jewelry. She's five-eight, and 125 pounds. She could use another 10 or 15 pounds. She's probably been losing weight for the same reason she hasn't been sleeping. She's very nervous to see you."

I soaked in Monica's description, providing myself with a permanent visual image to work from.

I asked Monica, "Anything else?"

She stood up and said, "No, that's it, except I think she's tired, scared, and really needs our help. And if you're not nice to her, you know I'll kick your butt!"

"Yes, ma'am," I said. "Please bring her in."

Monica asked on her way to the outer door, "Am I in or out?"

I thought for a minute and said, "Bring her in, and you stay with us. But no notes or recorders. Just listen and ask any questions you need clarified. I don't want to intimidate her any more than she already is."

Monica informed me, "There's a box of Kleenex in your upper, right-hand drawer."

I was a bit confused and let Monica know I wouldn't be needing them.

"She will," Monica said as she opened the door and invited Rebecca Ivers into my office.

ecky Ivers rushed across my office, around my desk, and hugged me tightly. I thought that Monica's assessment of her height-weight ratio was probably accurate as usual. Becky's voice quivered as she said, "Jake, thanks for agreeing to see me. I don't know what else to do. I simply don't have anyone else to turn to."

Monica got Becky settled in the left-hand client chair in front of my desk, and Monica settled into the one on the right.

Becky blurted out, "Jake, I'm sorry I've been so self-centered. I haven't even thought to ask how you've been. There have been so many things happening in my life over the last two years. With John gone and having to get the kids through college myself and deal with the business problems, I just haven't had much emotion to spare."

As I sat and listened to this middle-aged woman I had met almost 25 years ago, when we all had everything in front of us, I couldn't help but slip into the mind of that other Jacob Dyer of so long ago.

#. #. #.

After John and I somehow survived basic training, we started receiving the flight instruction that we would complete before going to Vietnam.

I remember the night John met Becky. He came back to the barracks, walking about two feet off the ground. He said, "Wake up, Okie. I have found the one!"

"Found what one?" I asked.

"My wife and the mother of my children," he stated with confidence.

"Does she know that yet?" I asked skeptically.

He said, "No, not yet. But, boy, you always get bogged down in the details. She's the one, and I'm as sure of it now as I will be 25 years from now."

We met her the next night at our favorite hangout, and I could certainly understand why John was as captivated as he was. She was young, beautiful, and had an infectious, positive outlook that pervaded everyone around her. It was hard not to feel upbeat when Becky was on the scene.

#. #. #.

Now, here I was 25 years later wondering what cruel twists life had taken to turn that bubbly, young, energetic beauty into this middle-aged, terrified, frantic woman in front of me.

I asked her, "Becky, what can we do for you?"

She sat there, nervously drumming her fingers on the armrest, and said, "I just don't know where to start."

She became even more emotional until Monica said calmly, "If you'll just start at the beginning, we'll get through this, and Jake will work everything out."

Becky and I both felt better, thanks to magnificent Monica.

Becky began explaining to us, in a halting monologue, how John had left the military and went into the air cargo and charter business with her father.

Becky's father, John's father-in-law Charlie Owens, was a World War II fighter pilot. He had a million stories and the ribbons and medals to back them up. Once Charlie had settled back into civilian life, he got one old plane and started the Lone Star Cargo and Charter Service out of Amarillo, Texas. The business grew over the next 30 years, and by the time John was ready to join the family and the business, the newly-named Lone Star Aviation was famous.

Becky went on to explain that after Charlie Owens died, John Ivers became the new president of the company. John loved to fly more than play executive, so the company slid a little during the '80s and on into the early '90s. In order to try to turn it around, John started doing business with the wrong kind of people.

"I tried to look the other way and pretend they weren't as bad as I knew they were, but over the next several years, it was obvious that we were in trouble. Then when John was killed in the crash in '96, I just didn't care any more."

Becky's voice was shaking. I wanted to do something, but I knew that Monica was already handling the situation. Becky got herself under control and started again.

"Now I'm absolutely broke, I'm in debt, the authorities are after the company, and I'm not sure anymore that John's death in the plane crash was really an accident."

I had always wondered about John's death, myself. From the moment I heard that he had been killed in a plane crash air freighting some oil field equipment down in Mexico, something simply didn't ring true. As fliers go, there are good pilots, great pilots, and John Ivers. I was with him when he flew in and out of situations that I still today would think impossible. I am alive now because of one of his most heroic aviation feats, although for years I wasn't in the least grateful that he had saved what was left of my life.

#. #. #.

We were on a routine mission doing some scouting along a winding river valley. We were just wrapping up the last sector, and I could almost taste the cold beer in the dim bar back at the base. The sun was glinting off the muddy river as it sliced through the dense jungle. The sights were beautiful and, in a permanent way, awesome. I had no idea that instant that they would be the last things I ever saw.

Then, out of nowhere, something hit us on my side of the chopper, and the whole world exploded. I could feel the downdraft from the rotors rushing over me and the blood dripping from my head, down my chest, and into my lap. I was surprisingly calm, especially considering the fact that I was certain we were dead. I remember feeling some relief in that we weren't going to be prisoners of war. There are some things that, at least in your mind, are worse than dying.

I heard John frantically calling into the radio that we had been hit and needed assistance immediately. I could feel that we were slipping laterally out of the sky, and I knew any moment, I would hear the sickening crash as we hit the jungle canopy.

Then I heard the words from John that I have praised and cursed alternately for over a quarter of a century. "Just hang on, Okie. Nobody's going to die on my watch."

Somehow, as the miracle was explained to me later, just as we were about to hit the trees along the river bank, we caught a gust of wind, and John momentarily stabilized our helicopter. He was able to hold it steady long enough to drift us over the jungle toward the mouth of the river where it dumped into the South China Sea. Somehow, he skimmed the top of the waves for a few more heroic minutes and was able to maneuver a partially-controlled crash landing onto the deck of a navy hospital ship anchored offshore.

I remember the two orderlies that rushed to get us out of the helicopter as it was beginning to burn. One asked the other, "Where did these guys come from?"

The other replied, "Either Heaven or Hell. I'm not sure."

Those words were to echo in my mind through the coming months of pain, agony, and suffering. In my darker hours, they are with me even today.

#. #. #.

I was jolted back to the present when I heard Becky cry, "They stole our business, ruined our name, and then they killed him. And now I have nowhere to go and nothing to do except unload on you."

At that point, Becky lost all control, and the anguish, the loss, and the grief combined to render her conversation useless for the time being. Monica handed her several of the Kleenex that she had predicted would be necessary and led her out of the room.

I realized that the only link to John and whatever had really happened was locked in the tortured mind of his grieving widow. I considered her pain in coming to grips with her husband's death in an accident while performing his job. There is at least some honor and sense in that; but when somehow you come face to face with the reality that his life had been taken from him by people whose only motive was to grab a few more dollars, at least in her mind, John had died another death, and she was suffering again. The old wound that had started to heal was ripped open once more.

Some time later, Monica came back and let me know that she had gotten Becky situated in a nearby hotel. Monica warned, "She's just exhausted. What with the emotional roller coaster she's on and the fact that she must have driven all night to get here from Amarillo, she'll probably sleep straight through until tomorrow morning. I told her to just take it easy and call us when she woke up tomorrow, and we would be ready to continue our meeting. You're going to have to take it easy, boss. She's running on empty and doesn't have much to spare emotionally."

I sat there and realized I didn't have any answers, but it was time to begin formulating the questions that would lead me toward repaying a debt which had been compounding interest for over 25 years. I could still hear John saying, "Well, Okie, sometimes you just gotta do the right thing. And maybe someday you can do something for me."

CHAPTER 5

Monica and I spent the rest of the day putting the final touches on the successfully-resolved case of the missing accountant. Although I was pleased about the positive resolution of the matter and the forthcoming sizable check, I couldn't get Becky Ivers out of my mind.

As the details began to unfold surrounding this case, I knew it would be far beyond our comfort zone. It simply wasn't the sort of thing that we got involved in at Dyer Straits Lost and Found; however, I sat back and thought about everything John Ivers had done for me and how far beyond his comfort zone it must have been for him.

\# \# \#

I woke up in darkness. At least I thought I was awake. I had no point of perspective. I tried to relax and recall where I was. The last thing I could remember was the helicopter being hit and everything in the world going black.

As I drifted in and out of semi-consciousness, I considered the possibility that I was dead. I remember being surprised to discover it really didn't bother me that much if I were dead. It didn't bother me nearly as much as the ordeal I had before me.

I could feel the sensation of swaying up and down. I was to learn later that it was my fourth day on the hospital ship. People with rubber-soled shoes scurried around me as I overheard someone at the edge of my hearing say, "No, there's simply nothing we can do. He'll never see again. There's just nothing left."

I knew beyond the shadow of a doubt, they were talking about me. I drifted back below the surface of consciousness and hoped it would all go away as some kind of terrible nightmare.

#. #. #.

As I sat in my office on the 14th floor of the Derrick Building remembering that day on the hospital ship, I broke out in a cold sweat and had the same feelings wash over me that I had felt 25 years before. There are some things that do not fade with age. They are simply always there as a marker. In my case, it was a grave marker which signaled the death of that Jake Dyer and started the odyssey that resulted in this Jake Dyer.

Monica breezed into my office and sat on the edge of my desk. In the unwritten rules that govern our working relationship, this was a signal of something partly personal.

"You okay, Jake?" she asked, trying to keep the concern out of her voice.

"Why do you ask?" I shot back a bit defensively.

"I thought this Becky Ivers situation might be tough because—well—you know."

I relaxed a bit and said, "Thanks, Monica. I'm okay. At least for now."

Then Monica totally shifted gears, turned up the emotional energy about ten notches, and informed me, "Well, since the Dyer Straits Lost and Found agency has successfully navigated through the treacherous waters of still another case, I have taken the liberty of arranging our customary celebratory dinner."

I leaned back and chuckled a bit as I said, "I was not aware that the celebratory dinner was an absolute, concrete custom."

Monica shot back indignantly, "Jacob Dyer, that's just the kind of thing you would miss if I wasn't here. Sometimes I think you forget how fortunate you really are to have me. You and I will be having dinner at the Eagle's Nest Lodge at eight o'clock. Emerson will be serving both the veal and quail this evening. He has made arrangements for the appropriate wine. Franklin will be picking us up. Do you want to be picked up here or at your apartment?"

I thought for a minute and said, "I think I would like to leave from here. I want to go over this Becky Ivers situation in my mind, and walking home to change and walking back will give me an opportunity to do that."

Monica warned, "You better have all of that off your mind by the time we leave for dinner. I've got some errands to run, then I will stop by home and transform myself into your drop-dead, gorgeous date for the evening, and be back here at seven o'clock."

I told Monica that would be fine. Actually, as I contemplated the evening, it was more than fine. Later, I heard the front doorbell ring as Monica left, and I sat in silence dreading the fact that the past was rapidly bubbling up to meet the present. I hoped that the old Jake Dyer could continue to rest in peace and the one I had become would survive what I feared was ahead.

I walked out of my office, crossed the reception area, and locked the door to Dyer Straits Lost and Found on my way out. I unfolded my collapsible white cane as I walked down the hall and rang for the elevator.

I was so focused on Becky Ivers' situation that I have no memory of walking the eight blocks to my apartment building. This always concerns me because, without my sight, I need all my other senses fully functioning to navigate through downtown congestion. I realized that I had crossed nine major streets and walked past hundreds of obstacles and other pedestrians, all without consciously thinking about what I was doing.

As I walked into the lobby of my apartment building, I folded up the white cane. Sometimes, I imagine it as a cobra that I take out for a short period, but I'm always relieved when I can fold it up and safely store it away for the next time.

I got onto the elevator and pushed the button for the twenty-second floor. That's the next-to-the-last button on the right for anyone who cares about such details.

The Plaza Apartment building is renowned as an example of the Art Deco architectural period that was prominent 60 years ago here in the oil patch. Money was so abundant, and the second and third generation oil barons had traveled the world to the extent that they wanted to recreate parts of London, Paris, and Rome here in Oklahoma.

My 22nd floor apartment is the envy of almost everyone I know. It offers what may be the best view of the downtown Tulsa skyline. I realize that this view is entirely wasted on me, but somehow I feel better just knowing it's there.

As I exited the elevator and walked toward the door to my apartment, my next door neighbor, Linda Taylor, opened her door. Either she opens her door a lot or always happens to be going in or out when I walk by.

Linda is about 30 years old, and I am told that her swim suit—or the lack thereof—is a tourist attraction at the apartment pool. Linda never seems to be working, and she has a steady stream of gentlemen callers. The rumor mill, which is alive and well here in the Plaza Apartments, has branded her as a high-priced hooker. I have no direct knowledge that this is true or false.

As I walked past her door, she linked her arm in mine and purred, "Hi, Jake. You got time for a drink?"

Linda has an unbelievably deep voice. I don't know if she does that on purpose or suffers from some kind of chronic sinus condition, but I have never felt totally comfortable with her advances. I guess it's the fact that I've never been sure if her interest in me is personal or professional.

As I pulled away, I said, "Linda, I am so sorry. I just have time to change clothes and get back to the office for a very important meeting."

She sounded slightly hurt as she said, "Maybe next time."

As I unlocked the door to my apartment, I heard myself say, "You never know."

My apartment, in addition to the seldom-used view, features hardwood floors, oriental rugs, and the smells of leather, suede, and fine cigars. It is one of the very few places on earth that I feel totally comfortable. I know where everything is to be found, and nothing ever changes. Some people would find this terribly boring. I find it to be a haven from the whole world which is constantly changing and moving around me.

I went into my bedroom and reached for the suit at the far right of my closet. I knew this was my *I'm-not-kidding-around-now* blue suit that cost me more than what would represent three-months' income for the majority of my adult life.

By 6:30, appropriately garbed for the evening, I was sitting back at my desk on the 14th floor of the Derrick Building. I eased open the window behind my desk and heard the traffic sounds in downtown Tulsa fading away for the evening. Tulsa is a city that has a very busy downtown area during the work day but becomes a veritable ghost town after the sun goes down.

At ten minutes to seven, her magnificence, Miss Monica, made her appearance. She was humming a fanfare as she entered my office and posed in front of my desk. This is a ritual we have to go through each time before we go out on any type of semi-social occasion.

Monica stated confidently, "Mr. Jacob Dyer, you are undoubtedly the most fortunate gentleman in North America this evening. I stand before you in a ravishing, evening-length, midnight black, silk dress. This particular garment features a plunging neckline that is extensive enough to fire the imagination, but stops short of being vulgar. To balance the image, it has a slit up the right side that is, indeed, memorable. I am wearing the long strand of cultured pearls given to me by my dear friend and employer. The hair is worn swept up to accentuate the pearls and the aforementioned neckline. All things considered, I would say it is a definite 10, thank you very much."

I also made a mental note that she was wearing a fragrance reserved for occasions such as this. I believe Monica has discovered that I have a hard time concentrating here in the office when that particular fragrance is prevalent.

I stood up and bowed slightly, and said, "Your highness, I am suitably impressed."

With that exchange completed, she took my arm, and we headed off for our evening of celebration.

One of the myriad talents that Monica possesses is her ability to take my arm and, in a social or business setting, discreetly assist me to the extent that rarely does anyone know I'm blind unless we intend them to.

As we exited the Derrick Building through the revolving door, I was greeted by Franklin, all-around gentleman of unlimited talents, and incomparable limo driver.

Franklin and I began our association several years ago when I resolved a particularly sticky situation for Mrs. Maude Henson. Maude is now 90 years old, going on 200. She is heir to one of the largest oil fortunes anywhere in the world. Her late husband left her an impressive array of worldly possessions which includes a Rolls Royce limousine and an endowment to compensate the perpetual services of Franklin. As Maude no longer ventures out of her 48-room cottage, she determined that, as a token of her gratitude for my discretion in handling the above-mentioned situation, Franklin's services should be available to meet the needs of Dyer Straits Lost and Found and Jacob Dyer, personally.

This is an arrangement that I have found very agreeable, and I believe Franklin does as well, although his English livery formal training has limited his display of emotion to only a low rumble that emanates from somewhere in his chest and a brief nasal sniff that he uses on certain occasions to be determined solely by him.

As Franklin opened the passenger-side rear door, he intoned formally, "Good evening, Mr. Dyer, and to you, Miss Monica."

Monica giggled as she said, "Good evening, Frankie." And I could hear her kiss him on the cheek.

Monica is the only human being allowed to express any casual sentiment toward Franklin. They have a totally unique relationship with their own set of rules that baffles me from time to time.

Franklin helped Monica into the back seat and reviewed his check list as he held the door for me. "Sir, I have taken the liberty of placing a bottle of Dom Perignon on ice as I understand that we are celebrating this evening. Honduran cigars have been placed in the humidor, and I hope you will find the London Symphony's version of Pachelbel's Canon in D Major acceptable for your listening pleasure. I assume since we have plenty of time before your dinner engagement, you would enjoy a detour through the peach orchard."

I smiled as I replied, "Perfect, as usual, Franklin."

He gave just a hint of the low rumble, and said, "Thank you, sir," as he closed the heavy Rolls door with a satisfying thunk.

The glorious strains of Pachelbel emanating from a multitude of hidden speakers greeted us as Monica poured the champagne into two fluted glasses. She offered a toast. "Here's to the good life."

I responded, "And the best people."

We clinked glasses, eased back into the leather seats, and as I sipped the nectar of the gods, I judged all was well with the world.

CHAPTER 6

ranklin piloted the Rolls Royce as we floated over the road out of Tulsa. Our destination was known as Eagle's Nest Lodge. It had been built before the great stock market crash as a hunting lodge for the idle rich who were profiting immensely from the burgeoning petroleum industry. The hunting lodge where these titans of industry would do battle with white-tailed deer and cottontail rabbits sat in the middle of a 5,000-acre tract of land which stretched from a huge plateau and bluff area all the way to the Verdigris River.

In the late 1980s, the lodge had been purchased by one of the new breed of business giants who make dollars spring forth from computer chips instead of a hole in the ground. The 60-year-old structure had been restored to its original grandeur, and one of the world's leading chefs was lured to Oklahoma and moved into the lodge where he prepares one meal each day for approximately 30 dining patrons.

As I was beginning to anticipate the culinary delights of Emerson's masterpiece, I felt the Rolls Royce turn off of the smooth highway onto a seldom-used black-top road that wound through miles of peach orchards.

I pushed a button on the panel in front of mè which slid open the sunroof, allowing the exquisite fragrance of peach blossoms to permeate the passenger compartment of the wonderful old Rolls Royce. As the magnificent machine swayed back and forth along the farm road, I was suddenly catapulted back to a hospital ship in the South China Sea.

#. #. #.

After the first of several operations to restore some semblance of order to my face, I was recovering in a crowded ward on the monstrous floating hospital. They had gotten me up and walking several times, so I had a general idea of where everything was located.

I waited until everyone aboard had settled down for the night and then slipped out of my hospital bed and stumbled my way down a corridor to the open foredeck of the ship. I felt my way along the rail and stopped, breathing in the tang of the ocean breeze.

Before I really thought about what I was doing, I stepped up on the first rail, balancing with my legs leaning against the top rail. I told myself it would be so easy. Just lean out, drift through space for a few moments, and allow all your problems to sink into oblivion.

#. #. #.

Franklin guided the limousine back onto the main highway, and I could feel us picking up speed. I checked my Braille watch and knew we would, as usual, be at the Eagle's Nest Lodge right on the dot of eight o'clock. I pushed the button which slid the sunroof closed.

Monica put her hand on my forearm and asked, "Where have you been?"

"Right here with you," I heard myself say hollowly.

"Not hardly," she replied. "I do hope you'll remember our rule about not discussing business at dinner."

My reliving the anguish on the hospital ship was all tied up with thoughts of John Ivers and the current problems with Becky. I decided to put a lid on all of it and try to keep it sealed until later.

Franklin negotiated the drive in front of the lodge and brought the Rolls Royce to a barely perceptible stop. He opened the door, and we stepped out.

I said, "Thank you for the detour through the peach orchard, Franklin."

He gave a brief rumble and replied, "My pleasure, sir. I'll be here whenever you're ready."

Monica took my arm, and we walked up the steps and into the lodge.

Chef Emerson greeted us at the door. "How are my two favorite patrons?"

Monica laughed and said, "You're so sweet, but tell me, who does this guy come here with besides me?"

Emerson chuckled, "Tonight along with your veal and quail, we will be serving a healthy portion of discretion, my dear."

Monica absolutely sparkled all evening. There are times in our lives that are simply magical. Nothing can interrupt them, and nothing can make them go wrong. That evening was one of those times.

Observing our rule to never discuss business at dinner, Monica and I steered the conversation from Dante's *Inferno* to the latest music from Elton John. She seemed to know quite a bit about most everything. The more I get to know Monica over the years, the more I realize that there's an awful lot I don't know. But it remains a pleasure discovering the hidden treasures.

After dinner, we strolled along the verandah upstairs. The breeze was cool, and there were at least a million crickets making themselves heard from the woods around the lodge. I lit the creation from one of Honduras's finest cigar rollers. I was grateful that Franklin had thought to bring the cigars along. Monica and I walked and talked, and time moved too quickly as it can only do when you are living one of the best of times.

Finally, I asked Monica, "Well, young lady, do you think I should get you home before you turn into a pumpkin?"

She replied, "I think you have your literary metaphors mixed up."

I told her it was the thought that counts as we walked down the wide stairs, arm in arm. Before we joined Franklin at the car, Monica and I observed one of our time-tested rituals which involves walking out onto what is known as the promontory. It is a group of rocks that juts out from the bluff and hangs in space over a 250-foot drop to the river below.

The breeze was much stronger on the promontory, and as I leaned against the rail, I was suddenly—once again—perched between life and death on a similar rail in the South China Sea.

#. #. #.

As the ship moved up and down, I was surprised that with no sight and no visual point of reference, I was able to keep my balance by simply leaning my legs against the upper rail while standing on the lower one. I was trying to decide if there wasn't something appropriate for one to say or do before ending it all. Realizing it simply didn't matter, I had just resigned myself to oblivion when I heard a voice behind me.

"Nice night, isn't it, Okie?" John commented lightly.

"Don't try to stop me!" I shot back.

"Now why would I want to stop someone from getting a little fresh air when I know they've been cooped up all day in the ward downstairs? I'm just barely able to get around on this leg they've been trying to piece back together, and I sure wouldn't want anyone to stop me from enjoying an evening like this," he said.

I confessed to John, "It's just not worth it any more. If it ever was. I would just as soon end it here."

"Well, old buddy, you may remember that we had us a deal that goes all the way back to basic training and our little picnic with Sergeant Sunshine. The deal was—and still is—that we get through this together, or we go down together. Now, I'm not sure I'm able to go over the top rail like you, but if you want to jump, I think I could squeeze through that second rail right behind ya."

That was the beginning of the end of the old Jake Dyer and the birth of what I have become. I didn't really care about saving my own life, but I knew John Ivers well enough to know if I went over the rail, he would follow me into the South China Sea.

Several nights later, back on the ward where John had somehow finagled his way into the bed next to mine, we had one of those conversations that can only take place in the depth of night just before the dawn.

"Would you have really followed me and killed yourself?" I asked.

"Jake, where I come from, a deal is a deal. I told you if you jumped, I would jump," he replied.

"You mean to tell me you would have thrown away everything, including your life with Becky, simply because we had a deal?" I asked.

John chuckled and then admitted, "Partner, I wasn't nearly as nervous about it as you might think. If you'd have gone over the rail, I sure would have jumped after you. But the way I had it figured, we both would have landed in a life boat tied off about eight feet below the rail."

I tried to calculate in my mind the debt you owe someone who goes through Hell with you when they could be somewhere else.

#. #. #.

As Monica and I joined Franklin at the limousine, I hoped I could gather up enough currency to pay off that old debt, and I knew the first payment was due the next morning when I would meet with Becky in my office.

## CHAPTER 7

The next morning at 5 a.m., I was tapping my white cane on the sidewalk as I did my daily commute to the Derrick Building. The magic of the Eagle's Nest Lodge the night before was a distant memory filed away to be brought out and savored again in the future. I was thinking about everything that had transpired with John and Becky Ivers and what, if anything, I could do to make a bad situation a little better.

As I rounded the last corner, I heard the morning News and Comment from Leroy Small. "Good morning, Mr. Dyer. Another hot one, I'm afraid. Interest rates may be going up, your president is taking a two-week vacation, and the mayor of our fair city fears that race relations may be at a 20-year low point."

"What did you do to mess up the race relations, Leroy?" I asked.

Leroy laughed and stated, "As a member of the oppressed, African-American race myself, I can assure you that I'm holding up my end in the race relations situation."

I replied with the first thing that came to my mind. "Leroy, if everyone walked around in the dark like I do, we wouldn't know the difference from black and white, and we'd just be forced to live with each other—for better or for worse."

Leroy laughed and gave me his parting commentary for the morning. "Jake, I do wish that everyone could see the world as clearly as you do."

Upstairs in my 14th floor sanctuary with the morning coffee and cigar ritual successfully underway, I leaned back in my leather chair and pondered the meeting with Becky planned for first thing this morning. I didn't know if I could formulate any answers. In fact, I wasn't sure where to find the right questions.

I put on a recording of a wonderful pianist rendering one of Bach's best efforts as I enjoyed my coffee and cigar. Johann Sebastian soothed my mind, and I mentally prepared for the ordeal to come.

At eight o'clock, earlier than usual, Monica breezed in and sang out, "Good morning, Jake. I'm going to save the bagels until Becky arrives. I called her hotel this morning, and she'll be in at about 8:30."

Monica sat on the edge of my desk and said, "Thanks for last night, Jake. It was wonderful, as always."

"We should do it again sometime," I suggested.

Monica stood up and moved to the right-hand chair in front of my desk and said, "You just let me know when the next time is, and your faithful companion will be ready."

She broke a prolonged silence by asking, "Well, boss, how do you want to handle this morning?"

I explained, "I don't know where to start. I don't even know *if* we should start. You know as well as I do this thing is out of our league. Maybe it would be better if someone else handled it."

Monica said, "She really needs us, and I don't think there's anyone else around to help her. Besides that, somehow, even more than she needs your help, I think you need to be a part of helping her."

The front bell had barely stopped ringing before Monica was up and escorting Becky into my office. She got Becky seated in the left-hand chair in front of my desk and offered her a bagel. Monica asked, "Would you like coffee?"

Becky sounded a bit hesitant but stronger than yesterday as she said, "Thank you. That would be nice."

Monica laughed and said, "I'm not sure it's nice, and I want to go on record right now and clarify that Jacob made this coffee. It has been known to peel paint and can be used to resurface parking lots."

Monica handed her a cup of my specialty. Becky took a sip and said, "It is definitely substantial."

"The breakfast of champions," I said confidently.

I broke the uncomfortable silence that threatened to linger when I said, "Becky, I know a lot about the company your father built as does everyone who has ever read a business magazine. I know that when John took over, it went downhill, and there were reports that the business might be forced into bankruptcy. I had talked to John a few times over the years, and he had let me know that things were really bad, and he didn't care much about the business. He just wanted to fly. Then I knew that business seemed like it was picking up just before he crashed."

Becky, resigned to the inevitable, spoke hesitantly. "About a year before John died, the business was at the end of its rope. The banks had threatened to shut us down. Our fleet of airplanes was getting old and badly in need of service. We had reached the point where we were not even going to be able to meet our payroll.

"Then, one of the bankers recommended John meet with Max and Jim Ed Leland. Later, I learned that they owned the bank and set up the meeting themselves by using one of their bank officers. They agreed to pay off all the debt and take control of the company that my daddy built. They said John could keep flying and have a token seat on the board.

"Well, we didn't have any choice, so John and I signed what seemed like dozens of contracts, releases, and I don't know what all. Little did I know that I had just signed John's death warrant."

Becky began crying softly but was in much better shape than the day before. I knew that she was a strong lady and was committed to dealing with her problems head on. She collected herself and continued.

"The Leland brothers are nothing but thugs. They immediately broke all of Lone Star Aviation's long-standing contracts with people who had trusted us through the hard times. Many of these relationships were built up by my daddy and were more than 30 years old. The Lelands just ran roughshod over everyone. And anyone that didn't agree to take it was threatened or coerced behind the scenes.

"Then they started splitting up what little business was left until Lone Star Aviation was nothing more than a front for something I don't understand. They leveraged everything that the company had left and bought a multi-million dollar jet that they use for nothing more than training runs. For some reason, when they bought the jet, they paid almost twice what it was worth. I never could understand who they were training when we had virtually no business left anyway.

"I've had several calls from federal agents regarding our corporate activities. I've told them all that I don't know anything about it, but apparently some of the paper work I signed makes me still responsible for everything.

"Just before John took that last trip, he told me he had discovered some things, and it all had fallen into place in his mind. He told me that when he got back, he was going to blow the lid off the entire thing. And that's when they killed him.

"At this point, I know I'm probably ruined financially. I would just like to clear my daddy's name and the name of Lone Star Aviation. And most of all, I want to clear John's name and make those animals pay for what they did to him."

I took it all in and then said with a degree of confidence that I didn't feel, "Well, Becky, it sounds pretty straightforward. We'll just come down to Amarillo and nose around a bit and see what we can find. It would probably be best if you headed home and acted like you don't know me until we get this resolved.

"I am going to draft a document telling everything I know and suspect about this matter, and if anything happens to me, my lawyer will send it to a friend of mine in the federal prosecutor's office.

"Monica will make all the arrangements, and we should be in Amarillo this time tomorrow."

Monica led Becky out of my office and let me know she would get her checked out of her hotel and on her way home.

I leaned back in my chair with a sense of dread and uncertainty but, at the same time, a knowing deep inside that the final piece of the puzzle that held my healing and inner peace lay somewhere in Amarillo, Texas.

CHAPTER 8

While I was contemplating what in the world we were going to do when we got to Amarillo, Monica scurried about for the rest of the day performing her magic preparing all the details for the trip and to have everything at the office covered while we were gone.

I slept fitfully that night as images of John and Becky, the South China Sea, and a jet tumbled through my brain. The next morning, at 6 a.m. sharp, as arranged, there was a tap at my apartment door, and I opened it. I heard the dignified voice of Franklin saying, "Good morning, sir. I will take your bag, and here is a cup of coffee Miss Monica informed me is for medicinal purposes."

As I sipped the coffee and he took the bag which I had packed the night before and placed beside the door, I tried to think of anything I might be forgetting. When you don't have any idea what you're doing, it's very difficult to come equipped with everything you might need.

As Franklin and I rode down the 22 floors in the elevator, he filled me in on the arrangements that he and Monica had conspired to bring forth.

"Sir, I have taken the liberty of renting transportation described as a sports utility vehicle. I felt that the Rolls might be a bit conspicuous in Amarillo. I have reserved three rooms in an establishment with the dubious name of the Armadillo Lodge. Please understand that I fear its only redeeming quality may be that it is close to the headquarters of Lone Star Aviation and the airport.

"The drive should take about six-and-one-half hours. I have packed an adequate supply of suitable champagne and cigars, and this morning, with your permission, we will be listening to a rousing selection from Vivaldi. Even though we are venturing into the wilderness, I see no reason that we should be uncivilized.

"Miss Monica asked me to pass along all of these details to you and let you know that your cinnamon raisin bagel with light cream cheese is on the back seat next to her. She asked that she not be awakened until a more reasonable hour. I believe she suggested closer to 9 a.m."

By the time Franklin had recounted all the arrangements, he opened the door and I slid into the back seat next to Monica. Franklin stowed the luggage, and Vivaldi serenaded us as we headed toward Amarillo, Texas.

It's important to understand that for someone raised in Oklahoma and for someone who has chosen to spend his life there, Texas is not a positive place. I have heard many

Oklahomans state that if God wanted to give the earth an enema, it would be applied somewhere in Texas. I'm quite certain Texans feel the same way about those of us who choose to live in Oklahoma.

The sports utility vehicle was nice, but it was certainly not the Rolls Royce. Nevertheless, I relaxed and began thinking about everything we were going to face in the days to come.

My mind carried me back to another long ride years ago.

#. #. #.

After several rounds of plastic surgery to reconstruct my face, the doctors on the hospital ship determined they had done all they could do, and John and I were transferred ashore and put on a bus to be taken for air transport back to the States. I have no idea how John always arranged to be in the same place at the same time I was, but I came to almost take it for granted that he would be there.

After the long, hot bus ride, we were dropped off at an air base and told that the next plane would not leave for at least ten hours. We were informed that with our low rank, it was likely that neither of us, or maybe only one of us, would get on the next air transport. We found what passed for a waiting lounge and settled in.

John's reconstructed leg was still giving him a lot of trouble, and he let me know he needed to take a short walk to keep it from stiffening up. As I sat there alone, wondering why I was continuing to play this ridiculous game as if I were going to go home and everything was going to be all right, I heard someone approach and sit down close to me.

I heard a raspy voice say, "Are you really blind?"

"That's what they tell me," I replied.

Then I heard someone rummaging through my bag, and it was drug across the room. I shouted, "Hey, that's my bag! Leave it alone! Put it back!"

I just heard the same, raspy voice, laughing.

I sat there, utterly helpless to control my environment or even my emotions. I wanted to cry, but I wasn't going to give the raspy-voiced thief that much satisfaction. About that time, I heard John's reliable, calm voice say, "You know, it can be confusing because all these G. I. bags look alike, and sometimes I've heard about a fella grabbing the wrong bag by mistake. Friend, I think that may have happened to you."

The raspy voice said, "Just stay out of it. It's none of your business. I'm base security, and I'm going through this bag."

John replied, "Friend, I don't care if you're the Dalai Lama, you put that bag down, or you'll spend the next few hours picking up your teeth one at a time. Now, if you think I'm kidding you, just don't have that bag back over here in the next ten seconds. You know, I was just explaining to one of the guys outside they need some entertainment around here while we're waiting on the next plane. Rearranging your dental work might be just what the doctor ordered."

At about that time, I heard my bag plop down next to my right shoe, just where it had been before.

John said, "Now I appreciate that, friend, and I think it would probably be best if you waited outside. It's a little bit close in this lounge."

The raspy voice complained, "It's 110 degrees in the shade out there, and there's no shade!"

John laughed as he explained, "Well, friend, I think that's just what you need. Your color doesn't look real good, and all that fresh air will help you to examine the difference between right and wrong. You can look forward to an afternoon of character building."

I heard the raspy voice mumble as his footsteps retreated out of the lounge.

John said, "Nothing like a little excitement. Now, I think I'll try and get some beauty sleep before our plane arrives."

What seemed like an eternity later, they came to tell us that the plane was refueling, but there was only room for one of us. A cold fear came over me as I considered the impossibility of traveling halfway around the world without John.

John laughed, stood up, and began walking across the room. He called back to me, "Sit tight, Okie. Let me see if I can get these people smoothed out."

Thirty minutes later, I was seated next to John on the front row of the military transport as it took off. I asked John how this stroke of good luck might have come our way.

He laughed and said, "You may not believe this, but there was a guy scheduled to sit in your seat who couldn't make the plane. It seems that he sat outside in the hot sun all afternoon and when it came time to climb the stairs to get on the plane, he was so disoriented and light-headed, he slipped and fell. But you'll be happy to know I made sure they got him carried off to the base hospital, and they'll be taking real good care of him."

My cold fear had faded away knowing that John would be by my side until we got home.

I said, "John, I don't know how to thank you."

As John drifted off to sleep, he said, "Maybe someday, Okie, you can do something for me."

# # #

As Franklin skillfully drove our sports utility vehicle across the high plains somewhere west of Oklahoma City, I began hearing small noises that indicated Monica was preparing to join the realm of the living. After a few coughs and mumbles, she croaked, "Coffee!"

I handed her what was left from my cup. She moaned, "This is cold, Jake."

I replied, "Yes, your highness. I am aware of the fact that your morning beverage is a bit chilled, but you must understand we are over three hours into our journey, and you have been comatose until this point."

Monica cheerfully called forward to Franklin, "Good morning, driver."

Franklin emitted a brief, low rumble and replied, "Good morning, Miss, and I trust everything is to your liking this fine day."

"My coffee's cold, and I'm having a sensation like an elephant standing in a rain storm."

Franklin gave out with a brief sniff which generally indicates varying degrees of disapproval as he questioned, "I beg your pardon?"

Recognizing a lack of communication and a situation that needed an interpreter, I broke in. "Franklin, I believe her highness would like us to locate a restroom and some hot coffee in the very near future."

Franklin seemed to have the situation resolved in his mind as he said, "Very good, sir. I suspected it was something of that nature; however, the elephant reference threw me off momentarily."

"Quite understandable," I reassured him.

Shortly thereafter, we got Monica properly fed and watered,

and we were underway again. I knew that our next stop would be the confusion, turmoil, and personal demons I would face in Amarillo.

CHAPTER 9

Franklin successfully navigated our sports utility vehicle to the Armadillo Lodge in beautiful, downtown Amarillo, Texas. As he pulled up in front of the office, Monica let out an audible sigh of resignation.

"I knew this was not going to be the Ritz-Carlton."

Franklin opened the door, and we stepped into the stifling heat of West Texas. As Monica took my arm, she said, "Tulsa's looking better all the time."

I cautioned her, "You should hold your judgment until we have an opportunity to hit all of Amarillo's high spots."

She laughed and said, "Everyone should have something to look forward to."

Franklin opened the office door, and we stepped in. Monica discreetly let me know that there was a counter straight ahead with a bored, high-school-aged young lady working the switchboard. There was a small seating area to the left and a display rack containing pamphlets and brochures from all of the area attractions.

I sized up the situation and said, "Franklin, why don't you see about getting us checked in, and Monica and I will peruse the available information about this fine city."

Franklin gave out a medium rumble and intoned, "Very good sir. I'll see to it."

Monica and I began going through brochures for western art exhibits, Indian reservations, and water parks. I could overhear Franklin's ordeal at the front desk.

"Young lady, we would like to check in. We have previously arranged for three rooms to be available."

She managed to get a tone of boredom into her southern drawl without interrupting her vigorous gum chewing. A very impressive feat if one follows that sort of thing.

"What was the name?" she asked.

"Franklin," came his curt reply.

"First or last?" she asked while continuing to mutilate her gum.

"First or last what?" Franklin seemed confused.

The young lady, now achieving an indignance reserved for anyone over 20 years old who has obviously forgotten what makes the world go 'round if, in fact, they ever knew, shot back, "Is Franklin your first name or your last name?"

Franklin replied, "Miss, when I'm working, it's simply Franklin."

The young lady was now intrigued. She said, "Oh, you're one of those one-name people. Kind of like Cher or Madonna."

Franklin let out with the full-strength sniff that implies

one is ignorant, uninformed, or barely worthy of being named among the human race. He shot back, "Not hardly, young lady. If you could just inform me as to what maneuvers I would have to complete in order to secure the three rooms I previously mentioned, it would be greatly appreciated."

At that point, I lost track of Franklin's ordeal as Monica nudged me with her elbow. She had just located a brochure about the Amarillo Airport with some information about Lone Star Aviation. She also found a map of the city and outlying areas, along with some demographic information from a booklet entitled *Welcome to Amarillo*. She was gathering up all of her resource material as Franklin rejoined us triumphantly.

He said, "Sir, if I may. I have cleared the way for us to establish residence in the three connecting rooms we discussed earlier. We are adjacent to one another on the second floor of this establishment, and I have been assured we have a delightful view of the back parking lot. I have taken the liberty of assigning you to the middle room and Miss Monica will be housed in the left-hand room which passes for the bridal suite in this particular facility. It costs seven dollars per night extra but boasts *a really cool heart-shaped bathtub*, I am assured."

We settled into our respective rooms, and Franklin unloaded the luggage as well as champagne, cigars, CDs, and a stereo. He also unloaded several other boxes of provisions and equipment that let me know that he and Monica had been hard at work planning this expedition.

After Monica and Franklin settled in, they both drifted into my room through the connecting doors for instructions. Monica laughed, "The heart-shaped bathtub is really unique, although there were two crickets in the bottom."

"It sounds romantic," I responded.

She sighed and said, "It seems to be working for the crickets."

I determined that we should take the rest of the day to get the lay of the land and try to come up with a course of action. We briefly reviewed the literature Monica had and decided Franklin should take our vehicle and reconnoiter the airport area and, specifically, the Lone Star Aviation facilities.

We decided he should be casual and not draw any attention to himself. I told him that if anybody questioned him, he should act like a tourist from London. He was concerned that as he had not been in London for quite some time, his accent might be a bit rusty. I told him not to worry as in this town anyone from east of Chicago would easily pass for London.

Monica, we agreed, should check out the area watering holes to see what information she could gather from the locals about Lone Star Aviation. I decided to stay in the room and place some discreet phone calls to get the ball rolling.

As it was nearly five o'clock in the afternoon, we agreed to undertake our individual tasks and meet back in my room at ten o'clock that same evening. We went to work with the confidence born only of people who have absolutely no idea what they are doing or how to go about it. I felt like Don Quixote, the champion of lost causes. Being helpless and hopeless, however, is a situation that I grew accustomed to a long time ago.

#. #. #.

When John and I arrived Stateside from Vietnam, we were both sent to a West Coast rehabilitation center. John managed to make his leg injury seem just bad enough that it justified a level of treatment that kept him with me at all times.

Our first day in the rehab center, I received my initial visit from my mobility instructor, Sharon—better known as Attila the Hun. It took me years to learn to appreciate, respect, and love her.

That first morning, she bounded into my room and with a disgustingly cheerful voice said, "Well, Jacob Dyer, I think it's time we should be up and moving about and learning how to take care of ourselves."

I asked skeptically, "Are *you* having trouble getting about and taking care of *yourself*, too?"

She managed a stern tone and said, "Look, Dyer, we can do this the easy way or we can do this the hard way, but you can bet your Army boots we're gonna do this. I haven't lost a patient yet, and I'm not gonna let you screw up my record, so can you try to have a decent attitude for me?"

I replied with more sarcasm than I felt, "I don't know if I'll do it for you, but for the sake of your perfect record, I will at least listen to whatever you've got on your mind."

She then explained to me that I had two choices for my mobility. One was a guide dog, and the other was to learn the use of a white cane. She let me know that training for either option began with the white cane mobility instruction. Then, if I wanted to try working with a dog later, we could examine that possibility.

I asked, "How long is all of this going to take?"

She responded mechanically, "The white cane mobility instruction will be twelve weeks, and then if you want guide dog training after that, it will be another two months."

I was in shock. "Do you mean it takes two months for you to train a dog to help me get around?"

She laughed as she replied, "No, the dogs are already

trained. But it'll take you eight weeks to learn how to work with him and that's only if you can match his intellectual level."

That began our daily verbal jousting as I tried to learn the skill of white cane mobility. Somehow, with Sharon pushing me and John by my side every step of the way, we began making a little progress.

#. #. #.

As I was mentally complimenting myself on the fact that I had come a long way, I remembered that I was sitting in the Armadillo Lodge in Amarillo, Texas with no idea how to accomplish settling a score from years gone by.

Over the years in the Dyer Straits Lost and Found operation, I have developed the telephone into one of my most effective tools. For me as a blind person, talking on the telephone is the great equalizer. I spend my whole life talking to people I can't see and judging subtle intonations or brief pauses. The sighted world relies on visual cues, so when I get one of them on the telephone, I have a distinct advantage. Or at least this is what I always tell myself.

I picked up the phone, dialed directory assistance, and asked for the main number for Lone Star Aviation. I dialed the number and was greeted by a bored-sounding young lady with an Hispanic accent. "Lone Star Aviation, may I help you?"

I swung into action with my best imitation of a West Texas drawl. "Little lady, this here is Dusty Rogers. I need to get fixed up with one of your airplanes 'cause me and some of the boys are gonna go shoot some birds on up in the panhandle there. So what kind of planes do you got?"

She seemed cautious, and replied, "Sir, I'm not sure we have any passenger planes available for your trip."

THE SOUND OF HONOR

I came back with, "Now, Missy, that's really amazing that you don't have any planes available when we want to go, because I don't recollect tellin' you when we were goin'."

After a long hesitation, she stammered as she said, "Sir, most of our work recently is cargo shipments, and we just don't have that many passenger planes available. Why don't you call someone else?" and she hung up the phone without allowing Dusty to even reply.

I waited a few moments, dialed the same number, and was greeted by the same young lady. With my polished, back-bay-Boston dialect, I intoned, "I am inquiring with respect to a cargo plane to deliver a shipment of polo equipment to Dallas. We are somewhat flexible on the time of delivery as we do not need the equipment until next month."

After a brief hesitation, the reply came back, "I'm sorry, sir. All of our planes are busy doing charter work for passengers, and we really don't do a lot of cargo work anymore."

I hung up the phone, leaned back on the bed, and pondered about a cargo and charter business that didn't seem to be available to do either cargo or charter work. I thought to myself, *Dyer, there's more here than meets the eye.* As I laughed out loud at the absurdity of my thought, knowing that there's more everywhere than meets my eye, I tried to make sense of the confusing bit of information about Lone Star Aviation.

As I was still focusing on the paradox before me, Franklin and Monica returned to report on their expeditions.

CHAPTER 10

s Monica slumped into one of the two so-
called easy chairs in my palatial room, she
said with mock anger, "Jacob Dyer, you
told me years ago that if I would come to
work with you, I would see the world, experience the finer
things of life, and know a joy that few mortals ever achieve. I
hope that Amarillo was not what you had in mind."

I laughed and replied, "Young lady, do you know how many
people go through their whole life and think they've done it
all, but they missed everything that Amarillo has to offer?"

One of the things I appreciate most about my multi-talented,
capable colleagues is the fact that they match their mood to
mine. We can be the best of friends or the most intense of
co-laborers and, until recently, I was unaware of the fact that
Monica and Franklin always follow my lead.

I took a deep breath and said, "Let's try to figure out where we are. Why don't we start with you, Franklin?"

Franklin said, "I first took a perimeter tour of the Amarillo Airport complex. It is a small, commercial airport that only serves a handful of regional airlines, with the exception of major carriers like American which has shuttles to their hub in Dallas. Then I parked in an area known as charter row. This is where all the private planes, charter, and cargo services are located. I unfolded a map that Miss Monica had provided for me and slipped on a jacket and tie for my lost Londoner routine as you suggested."

Monica interrupted with a question. "Frankie, why the jacket and tie?"

Franklin gave a satisfied rumble and replied, "My dear, there is a saying that only mad dogs and Englishmen venture out into the midday sun. Somehow I felt the jacket and tie would fit this motif.

"I inquired of several gentlemen of limited vocabulary and dubious grooming habits where I might locate Lone Star Aviation. They all seemed to be shocked that anyone wanted to know about Lone Star. I deduced from their passing comments that at one time Lone Star was a premiere operation, but now they utilize what was described to me as *flying buzzards*, I believe was the phrase."

I interjected, "A bit crude, but it does provide a vivid visual image."

Franklin replied, "I guess it would, sir."

Franklin went on to explain that he had slipped in and out of several hangars that had Lone Star aircraft, mostly medium-sized propeller planes that seemed to be approaching the point of becoming antiques. No one at Lone Star seemed particularly concerned to have this wandering Englishman in their midst until Franklin approached a new hangar which was set off by itself at the very end of charter row.

Franklin explained, "As I approached the new hangar, I could barely make out the tail section of a beautiful, new jet. Later one of the other mechanics down the row informed me that it was a King Jet, and it must have cost millions of dollars.

"Apparently, Lone Star keeps very tight security on the King Jet hangar. I got within 50 feet of the door when I was abruptly asked to leave. I gave them my story about being across the pond from London and just here to visit the colonies, don't you know."

Monica laughed and asked, "And what did they say, handsome?"

Franklin replied with an indignant sniff, "He called me a limey idiot and told me if I couldn't be off the premises in ten seconds that they would help me exit."

I had learned quite a bit from Leroy Small and his morning News and Comment about King Jets. It seems that about a year before, the honorable Governor of Oklahoma had acquired a King Jet and had been called on the carpet by the legislature for misusing this official new toy. The legislature, particularly the opposition party, had claimed that a King Jet is a multi-million dollar extravagance for cross-country travel. Our Governor, they felt, needed to be spending all of his time in Oklahoma. They went on to accuse him of using the jet for unofficial business such as hunting, fishing, and attending football games. I always felt that the legislature had overlooked the fact that, historically, the main duties of Oklahoma's Governor include hunting, fishing, and attending football games.

Franklin went on to explain that he had stopped by a couple of other small carriers on the way out but did not learn anything else of significance until he stopped at the control tower.

Franklin explained, "I got a clipboard out of our vehicle—very handy device, those clipboards—and strolled into the control tower as if I were Bonnie Prince Charlie, himself. I explained to the supervisor that I was on brief holiday from my employment as an air traffic controller in Liverpool, and I wanted to determine how you Yanks were doing things in ways we might not yet have discovered."

"Very nice," Monica purred.

Franklin let out with the satisfied rumble and went on to tell us that, in a roundabout way, he had learned that Lone Star Aviation's King Jet was only used every other day for a four- to five-hour training run. They always filed a flight plan to do practice landings and refuel somewhere this side of the Mexican border, and then they promptly returned to Amarillo. The plane was always kept under tight security in the far hangar which was brightly lit at night.

Franklin had also stopped by airport security and, after posing as a brother security officer from Gatwick Airport in London, learned that all people and/or cargo for Lone Star Aviation came and went in black vans without windows. Therefore, it was difficult for anyone to know what was going in or out, and since they were only training flights for new pilots, there's really no paperwork or documentation required."

"Nice job, Franklin. I'm not sure what all that means, but you performed just as I expected," I said.

"Thank you, sir," Franklin replied with his predictable rumble.

Monica knew it was her turn to report, but she always likes to be asked. I believe she feels it builds up the proper amount of suspense and gives her a good introduction. Since she knows how to make an entrance better than anyone I have ever met, I always indulge her.

"And now, Miss Monica, would you grace us with the details of your findings?"

Monica replied with what I felt was an appropriate appreciation for the introduction. "Thank you, sir. You will be happy to know that the highlight of Amarillo night life and one of the top places that the society and business giants gather is called the Road Kill Lounge which, coincidentally, is located off the lobby of our very own Armadillo Lodge."

Monica explained how she had been very low profile during her evening in the Road Kill Lounge. Monica has never been low profile, and I'm certain that the Road Kill Lounge will never be the same, but I didn't feel that it was the time to bring it up.

Monica continued, "The bartender, Larry, is a real nice guy. He gave me free drinks all night because his mother's name is Monica. I know it sounds absurd, but you can't look a gift horse in the mouth. My new friend, bartender Larry, let me know that Lone Star Aviation was just a skeleton of what it used to be. He referred to it as being like the Pony Express. I asked him about Max and Jim Ed Leland. He turned about four shades of red, and in a confidential tone, suggested that people who were concerned about their health didn't mess around with the Lelands."

I asked, "Didn't this guy get a little concerned about all your straight-forward questions about Lone Star and the Lelands?"

Monica giggled and said, "Trust me, boss. I know how to handle guys like Larry. I can assure you at no time during the evening was his mind on Lone Star Aviation or the Leland brothers. He was zeroed in on what you might call the stuff that dreams are made of."

Franklin gave a rumble of appreciation for a job well done as Monica continued.

"I did learn that if you want to know about the glory days of Lone Star Aviation and how they got from there to here, the guy you need to talk to is Colonel Deke Sawyer. Deke Sawyer is a retired Air Force flyer. He has been with Lone Star Aviation for over 20 years. He was there when Becky's father, Charlie Owens, ran the business back in the days when it was a legendary operation. I found out that Deke Sawyer frequents the Road Kill Lounge and comes in most nights around nine o'clock. Larry pointed him out to me just before I left."

Monica described Deke Sawyer as early 60s and someone who had probably seen better days. Monica told me that men come in three flavors: those who aren't anything, but expect to be something someday; those who are resigned to be where they are; and those who used to be something but have faded. Deke Sawyer, she assured me, was squarely in the latter category. From just a brief glance, she surmised that his military career and his early days at Lone Star had been his highlights, and now he was simply hanging on to the past.

I tried to take in all I had heard from Franklin and Monica, but so many things simply didn't add up. We agreed that the next day Franklin should approach the local law enforcement authorities with a story about being an insurance investigator doing some background checks on Lone Star before writing a policy. Monica would spend the day at the library going through back issues of local newspapers, and I would *let my fingers do the walking* with some telephone inquiries. We planned to all meet for dinner the next night and compare notes before Monica and I arranged an accidental meeting with Colonel Deke Sawyer in the Road Kill Lounge.

As an old Army sergeant once told me, "Sometimes the best plan there is, is the one you got."

This was on my mind as Monica and Franklin retired for the evening, and I tried to clear my mind and find the sanctuary of sleep.

## CHAPTER 11

The terror would not subside. Cars, trucks, and buses sped by me, mere inches away. I couldn't get my bearings and knew any minute I would be crushed to death under one of the vehicles racing by me. I wanted to curl up into a fetal position and cry or, better yet, drop dead right where I stood and be done with it all.

The fear and intimidation of navigating as a blind person through a large and unfamiliar city for the first time is hard to describe to anyone who hasn't experienced it. I stood there for what seemed like hours, but I knew it was only a few moments. Then I heard Sharon's voice from behind me say, "You know what to do. We've practiced this before."

Just as I was preparing to scream at her, letting her know in no uncertain terms we had never practiced anything that had remotely prepared me for this, I heard John's calm voice say, "Well, Okie, a bit of a sticky situation here, but we've been through things worse than this back in Nam. I'd suggest you take a deep breath and trust your own judgment here. If you get through this successfully, I'll buy us a couple of beers when this is over. And, if you don't, I'll drink them both myself."

I waited until I heard the traffic patterns of the cars stopping at the red light. When the sounds around me told me that it was my turn to cross the street, I felt the curb with my cane and stepped off. Just then, I heard a horn blaring as the engine noise of the truck bearing down on me grew louder and louder.

#   #   #

I woke up in a cold sweat. That nightmare had remained with me for two-and-one-half decades. Although I knew every nuance of the scene that unfolded almost nightly, the terror never lessened.

As I threw back the covers and sat up, I had that realization that can come over you when you instantly become aware of the fact that you're in an unfamiliar bed in a strange place. But almost instantly, I remembered that I was in the motel room, and the world began to settle back into its normal pattern.

I stumbled about the room for a few minutes and sat down in one of the chairs. My Braille watch told me it was 3:45 in the morning. I was restless, but since I had not become familiar with anything outside of my room, I was stuck because I didn't want to wake up Monica simply to go for a walk just to calm my nerves. I knew beyond the shadow of a doubt that I could call her and nonchalantly ask if she would like to go for a walk, and she undoubtedly would have understood my innermost thoughts as she always does and acted like she was just waiting for someone to call her at a quarter to four in the morning to go for a stroll. Somehow just knowing that you can call on someone is almost as good as calling them.

The room that just a few minutes earlier had seemed like a claustrophobic jail cell, now seemed less threatening as I settled back into bed and slept until morning.

There was a knock on the outer door of my motel room at 8 a.m. As I would have expected Monica or Franklin to knock on their connecting doors into my room, I couldn't imagine who was outside. I opened the door and heard the first rumble of the morning.

"Good morning, sir. Miss Monica and I have taken the liberty of seeking out suitable bagels for the morning, and we have brought you several cups of coffee as well."

Franklin stepped in, followed by Monica who sounded surprisingly chipper for that hour of the morning.

"Good morning, boss. It's 8 a.m., and the temperature here in Amarillo, the garden spot of West Texas, has already reached 87 degrees, with a high expected at 104. The humidity is not to be believed, so I think we should change the subject."

I laughed and replied, "Monica, you're turning into a regular morning person. The next thing I know, you'll be getting up to experience the sunrise."

Monica said, "If God wanted me to see the sunrise, he would have arranged it for a bit later in the day; but if you're ever up in the middle of the night with nothing to do, I would enjoy having an escort to walk a poor, defenseless young lady around this Western town when it's not so hot."

I stood there and wondered if Monica had heard me

stumbling around in the night. Just when I think I have started to understand the depth of the princess, she surprises me once again.

Franklin had arranged our breakfast on the table. He and I took the chairs, and Monica perched on the corner of the bed. As we ate our breakfast, we reviewed the strategy for the day.

I began by saying, "It seems to me we need to start finding some answers to a lot of disconnected questions. For example: One, why does the struggling Lone Star Aviation not want any new charter or cargo business? Two, why have they let their entire fleet become rundown and dilapidated while going out on a limb for a multi-million dollar King Jet that they only use for training but keep under maximum security? Number three, who are Max and Jim Ed Leland, and why did they take over a struggling cargo and charter service and let it fade into just a shell or front? Number four, what did John Ivers discover, and what did they do to him? Number five, how can we stop whatever's going on and deal with whoever needs to be dealt with while saving the company and its reputation for Becky Ivers?"

We determined that Monica's trip to the library should focus on the Lelands, including their activity prior to Lone Star Aviation and how they took over the company. Franklin's insurance investigation with the local law enforcement agencies would zero in on the Lelands as operators of Lone Star and the company's mysterious activities.

I would make a call to a friend of a friend with the federal prosecutor in Oklahoma City and find out how we could expose the Lelands and take them down without harming Becky or what was left of Lone Star Aviation. We didn't want to throw out the baby with the bath water.

Franklin planned to drop Monica off at the library as he would need transportation for the day. We agreed to meet back in my room at four o'clock that afternoon to compare notes and change for dinner. My thought was we could relax over dinner and plan the best way to use whatever information we may have gained. After dinner, Monica and I would arrange to bump into Deke Sawyer in the Road Kill Lounge at around nine o'clock. Franklin removed the debris left from breakfast as Monica retreated to her room to prepare for the day.

After a significant rumble, Franklin said, "Sir, you will want to know that the Narrative Television Network is on channel 17 here in the motel. In the boxes in the left side of your closet, you will find some of your books on tape, an abbreviated collection of music, and the portable stereo. Your cigars are in the traveling humidor on your dresser, and I have been informed that this establishment offers a limited room service menu for lunch."

He let his feelings about the Armadillo Lodge be known with a brief sniff as he described the room service possibilities.

A few moments later, I heard both Monica and Franklin close their doors and retreat down the stairs to face their individual tasks for the day. I settled back into my chair and considered how I might best make myself useful.

Thoughts of a multi-million dollar jet, Max and Jim Ed Leland, and Lone Star Aviation shuffled themselves through my brain. The question that shouted out to be answered was: *What did John Ivers know, and why did it get him killed?*

I realized, once again, how many times in my life John Ivers had been there for me to provide the missing elements I needed to keep me going. I knew that if I could spend just five minutes talking with John, this entire puzzle would fall into place, then

I could focus on taking this situation that had gone so wrong and, somehow, make it right.

But John wasn't here and he never would be again, so I had to find out what he knew. This was intimidating for me, because I had spent so many days when I couldn't understand anything, and John Ivers knew everything about the world around us, what to do next, and even my innermost thoughts.

Thinking about John led me back into my nightmare.

#. #. #.

The sound of the truck's constant horn and its roaring engine created a visual image in my mind of a fire-breathing dragon prepared to run me down and consume me. I dropped my cane, turned away from the oncoming sound, and covered my ears. My fate was sealed.

I remember thinking *I wonder why it hasn't killed me yet* when the truck roared past in the other lane. I stood there realizing that I was in the outer lane of a four-lane intersection, and the truck had been in the inner lane. I rushed back to the sidewalk, tripping over the curb, and sprawling onto the concrete. Tears coursed down my face, and I shouted, "Get me out of here! That's it for me! I will never do this again! I cannot believe you allowed me to get myself into this kind of situation."

Sharon put her hand on my shoulder as I slowly got to my feet. She said, "You were doing fine. You really didn't make any bad mistakes until you panicked and dropped your cane. You had timed the traffic perfectly and could have made it across the street."

I turned to her and said, "Well, you'll have the satisfaction of knowing that you taught me good timing, but that's all the satisfaction you're going to have, because you just lost your first patient."

Then I heard John's voice from behind me say, "Now, Okie, before we throw in the towel on this thing, I think we need to have a brief conference. I've been beside you every step of the way, and I think we're just about to lick this thing."

I whirled around to face him and shouted, "What do you know about it? It's real easy to stand there and calmly take in all the sights while I'm fighting for my life here. You have no idea what this is like."

Sharon put her arm back on my shoulder and said in a caring tone I did not know she possessed, "Jake, if you want to quit, that's your business. But you do need to know John's been with you every step of the way and not just taking in the sights. He arranged with me to have a bag placed over his head so that he could go through everything you are going through. That truck was honking at a man crossing the street in front of you with a bag on his head."

CHAPTER 12

The day stretched out before me. I tried not to think about the fact that I had seven hours to try to fill productively without going crazy. With Monica and Franklin about their daily tasks, I was once again stuck in the confines of a strange motel room where everything outside my door was No Man's Land.

I wanted to give the federal prosecutor's office in Oklahoma City until about eleven o'clock before I called them. It has been my experience when dealing with bureaucrats, even high level ones, that it is hard to get their attention first thing in the morning, but if you will call just before lunch or quitting time, their work has piled up and they have their minds on getting out of the office. That is the best scenario under which to request favors or slide by a shaky explanation of who you are and what you want. Therefore, I knew I had two hours to fill before the ideal time to place my call.

I found the remote control on my bedside stand and prepared to find out what the television might have to offer me. The Narrative Television Network makes movies and television accessible for blind and visually impaired people. They add the voice of a narrator in between the dialogue of characters in a show so that I or any blind person can enjoy movies or television.

I turned on the TV in my motel room and quickly found channel 17 exactly as Franklin had indicated I would. I enjoyed narrated versions of two of my favorite classic detective shows, *The Streets of San Francisco* and *Law & Order*. While it cleared my mind and kept me occupied until it was time to make my call, I couldn't help but think that Becky Ivers would be better off if she had Lt. Mike Stone or Lt. Anita Van Buren helping her instead of me.

Don Burns had been a great friend of mine. We had been in Vietnam together and after his tour, which he survived intact, Don settled in Oklahoma City, finished law school at night, and began working in the federal prosecutor's office. I used to think about why Don came through the war whole and I was left in the dark.

That line of reasoning permanently disappeared from my mind the day the Murrah Building blew up in Oklahoma City, and Don was gone. At his funeral, I talked with Bob Arnold who had been a colleague of Don's and had been with us briefly in Vietnam. He told me that Don had spoken of me often, letting him know that I was *one of the good guys*. Bob had assured me if there was ever anything he could do for me, he would certainly do his best to get it done.

I dialed the federal prosecutor's office in Oklahoma City after memorizing the number that a stressed-out young lady at Directory Assistance had given me. After talking to no less than five separate individuals in three different departments, I finally heard Bob's voice come on the line. "Jake, is that you, or is this a bad dream?" Bob chuckled.

"You can decide at the end of this call," I replied.

"What can I do for you?" he asked.

I explained, "I have a friend in trouble. Actually, you met her husband, John Ivers, when we were all in Nam together."

After a brief pause, Bob came back with, "Yeah, I remember Ivers vaguely. We didn't spend a lot of time in the same place, but he seemed like a good guy. How's he getting along these days?"

"That's what I want to talk to you about," I explained.

I told Bob how Becky had come to see me and how her father's business had been taken over by John and had gone through some tough times. I explained how, in desperation, John had made a really bad deal with Max and Jim Ed Leland and ended up dead. Bob knew about Max and Jim Ed, and his opinion was not flattering. He told me that the Feds' Racketeering and Organized Crime Unit had been trying to nail them for years, but, apparently, Max and Jim Ed were pretty slippery.

I told Bob that the only activity around Lone Star of any significance seemed to be the King Jet that was apparently used exclusively for some kind of training. Bob wondered why Lone Star needed to train pilots if their business was dwindling down to nothing. I assured him I didn't know, but it was one of the multitude of things I wanted to find out.

Bob told me he would root around by making a few discreet calls and checking the computer and get back to me. Before he hung up, he asked, "Jake, are you in deep on this deal?"

"I am in all the way," I replied.

He asked, "What's your angle?"

I explained, "There's an old debt that started way back when we were in Vietnam that has grown over the years. In fact, it feels like the national debt, and if I can clear Lone Star's name, clear John Ivers' name, put the Lelands away, and give the company back to Becky so she can begin to build it back, somehow I feel that the debt will be canceled."

After a long pause, Bob said, "Jake, that is a long shot at best."

I replied, "Bob, sometimes you just gotta do the right thing and hope that maybe, someday, someone will do something for you."

Bob ended the call with, "Give me a couple of hours."

I called the front desk and asked for Room Service and inquired as to the selections that might be available for someone desirous of a light luncheon. The young man who answered the phone in the midst of some tremendous background noise in the kitchen, told me that the menu was in my room.

Having no desire to explain my life story to this individual, particularly the part about being blind and not being able to read his wonderful menu, I told him how a stray dog had gotten loose in the parking lot. I was holding him for the dog pound people here in my room when, believe it or not, that dog ate my Room Service menu—seeming to enjoy it, by the way. I let him know that the dog had been safely picked up by the authorities, but the maid had not been able to supply me with a replacement Room Service menu, so I would be eternally grateful if he would give me a feel for the selections he was offering for lunch.

After a long pause, he asked, "Do you mean you want me to read you the menu?"

I explained, "Young man, I believe you are management material. On my next visit here to the Armadillo Lodge, I will be shocked if you're not running the entire place."

After a complicated exchange, I ordered a Caesar Salad and a Southwest Chicken Sandwich. When I asked the young man if the Southwest Chicken was a regional selection, he replied, "Oh, no, sir, we will bring it directly to your room."

Definitely management material.

I leaned back against the pillows at the headboard of the bed and thought about Bob Arnold and what he might be able to do for me. We had almost nothing to go on, and we were dealing with some people that definitely played for keeps.

I sat in my room and went through my regular ritual of experiencing my environment. This is a skill that has been developed over 25 years, and it has kept me sane and given me a quality of life that few people could imagine.

#. #. #.

John and I had survived our encounter at the intersection with the demonic truck. In one instant, I had hit bottom and started up. I had been drowning so long in my sea of despair, I didn't know how deep I was or whether I had what it took to get back to the surface, but, with John by my side, I had to try.

We began taking long walks together through the neighborhoods and along the beach. We got to the point that we would leave Sharon behind and venture out on our own. I remembered telling John, "Every time I feel scared or helpless or awkward, I simply tell myself, no matter how inept I feel, it could be worse. I could be like you, walking around with a bag on my head."

John laughed and said, "Okie, one of the most important things in this world is style. Now, a lot of people can do some things with style, but it takes real greatness to walk around with a bag on your head and manage to display a full portion of style."

Somehow John did it, and I can remember sitting atop a bluff over the Pacific Ocean with John at my side the day he started me on the road toward the wonder of experiencing my environment. John tried to seem casual as he began a dissertation I knew he had prepared and rehearsed many times.

He said, "Okie, most people walk around with five senses and don't have a clue what's going on. They are able to hear, but they don't listen. This bag has taught me that senses are no more than a method to get the information you need to get by, and I have discovered that with this bag over my head, there is more information available to me—or at least I'm aware of it in a different way—than if I didn't have the bag.

"Now, if I'd come out here with you without this fashionable designer bag atop my head, I would have seen the Pacific Ocean and everything around us. But an hour from now, I couldn't have told you which way the wind was blowing or how strong, what kind of sound the gulls make, how fast the waves are rolling in, or the texture of this grass and sand we're sitting on.

"This walking around in the dark is a bad thing, Jake. I'm not gonna lie to you. But somehow I feel like if you can ever get to the place where you live in the very center of what I'm talking about, you'll find a whole new world out there that most folks don't know anything about."

My education was to continue for a long time to come. For years, I had wondered how I could ever pay the tuition for that education that began at the Pacific Ocean. The day that Becky Ivers walked into my office, I knew how I might pay the tuition, and I knew that somehow, someway, I had to do the right thing.

CHAPTER 13

y Room Service lunch arrived in what I thought was a reasonable time if I had ordered it from Chicago, but it was edible. After lunch, I stacked all of my dishes and utensils back on the tray, opened the motel door, propped a chair against it, and set the tray outside my room.

I remembered an occasion when I had tried to accomplish this maneuver without propping a chair against the door and found myself locked out of my room. This was not something I even wanted to contemplate since I had no working knowledge of anything outside my second-floor room in the Armadillo Lodge.

As I turned to step back inside, I noticed how oppressive the heat and humidity were, and I smiled, anticipating Monica's outlandish account of surviving the inhospitable weather. I replaced the chair and closed the door.

I opened the traveling humidor Franklin had placed on my dresser. I took out a cigar and smelled it. I instantly identified it as one of the Ecuadorian brands that Franklin knew I enjoyed. It was seven-and-one-half inches in length with a ring gauge of fifty-two. After consulting my Braille watch, I calculated that my Ecuadorian companion, smoked sparingly, would stay with me the two hours I had to wait before Monica and Franklin returned from their expeditions.

As I lit the cigar and enjoyed the first few puffs, thanking heaven and an unknown artist somewhere in Ecuador, my phone rang. I picked it up and said, "Good afternoon, Bob."

Bob asked, "Does that motel have some kind of audio caller ID for blind people?"

I explained to Bob that although I had such a device at home that worked perfectly, the Armadillo Lodge did not offer such appointments. I told Bob that here at the Armadillo Lodge, hot water and clean towels are about all that could be expected.

Bob laughed and said, "Jake, that's one thing I appreciate about you. You always go first class."

I replied, "Well, when in Rome, you do as the Romans do. Have you found out anything for me?"

Bob took a deep breath and started. "Jake, my best advice after checking into the Leland brothers and their activities is to tell you to get out of there now and forget this whole thing. But since I know you're not going to do that, I'll try to fill you in briefly.

"The first thing I did after we talked was run a computer check on Max and Jim Ed Leland and Lone Star Aviation. There are a bunch of investigations that lead to the Lelands but nothing concrete that anyone can stick them with yet. Several of the investigations refer to Lone Star but only as background information in the Leland matters.

"Max and Jim Ed have been indicted a number of times, but we just can't put them away. They are well-connected and seem to always be one step ahead of us. We had Jim Ed wrapped up on a homicide, but the one witness that was ready to testify disappeared and a number of the good old boys, including a state senator, claim they were duck hunting with Jim Ed at the time. And Jake, that's about it from the official record."

"How about the unofficial record?" I asked.

There was a prolonged silence on the line, then Bob said quietly, "Our telephone conversation just ended. From this point forward, I have no recollection of any communication with one Jacob Dyer.

"The things that we know but can't prove involve the Lelands being behind drug trafficking and transporting illegals through Mexico. Unfortunately, there's not enough evidence to get warrants or even conduct an official investigation.

"And, Jake, this is so far off the record you wouldn't believe it, but the word has come down from on high to leave the Lelands alone unless you can guarantee a conviction. Apparently, Max and Jim Ed contribute huge money to some politicians. These politicians have let all the federal offices know that they're tired of having their honorable, upstanding constituents harassed. Therefore, anyone who points a finger at the Lelands risks his career unless he has enough to put them behind bars for sure."

I asked him about the mysterious operations at Lone Star Aviation and the suspicious security around the King Jet. I said, "Bob, there is no logical explanation for what's going on, and with the snakes we're dealing with, you know as well as I do that Max and Jim Ed Leland are dirty. They weaseled their way into Lone Star Aviation by defrauding John and Becky Ivers, then they set up shop using Lone Star as a front for trafficking in drugs and illegal aliens. When John caught on to it, I believe they had him killed."

Bob shot back, "Jake, you better listen to me, and listen good. These boys play hardball in the big league. A lot bigger league than you or I. And I want you to understand that unless you bring me all the evidence necessary to convict these people wrapped up in a nice, neat package with a pretty bow on it, there's not one thing I can do to help you. And if you start poking around this hornet's nest, you are going to get stung and stung very hard, and unfortunately, without concrete evidence I won't be able to help you. Not even one little bit. Do we understand each other?"

I pleaded, "Listen, Bob. They cheated some good people and killed my best friend, and you know as well as I do what they're doing."

Bob replied in a very low and resigned tone, "Jake, you can't prove anything. The King Jet has only been used for training runs and the other, older planes that Lone Star has are not profitable. But there's nothing wrong with that. It's not illegal to acquire a company and then financially run it into the ground. Jake, I'm sorry, but the next time I want to hear from you on this thing is when you've got all the goods on the Lelands or you've come to your senses and given up."

I heard a click on the other end as Bob disconnected our call.

I felt like a kid at a magic show who knows the magician is tricking him, but the magician just won't let him see the trick.

Knowing something and proving something are two different things, especially proving something to federal agents who have been warned to lay off the Lelands.

Just as I had predicted, as my Ecuadorian cigar was on its very last ashes, Monica and Franklin returned. They each took one of the chairs, and I remained propped up on the bed. As expected—and appreciated—Monica went to great lengths to describe the heat and humidity as well as the effect it had on her, her clothes, and—most particularly—her hair. She was just describing how this weather had entirely ruined her look when Franklin rumbled and said, "May I say, young lady, that you are, indeed, the loveliest sight I have encountered since we arrived in Texas."

I responded with, "Franklin, you always have been one to display the most discriminating taste."

Monica thanked us both, and we got down to business. I decided to get a report from Franklin first to see if his inquiries to the local law officials mirrored the response I had received from Bob Arnold at the federal level.

Franklin reported, "I met with several members of the local constabulary, including two deputies, the county sheriff, as well as the chief of the Amarillo police. They all seemed to accept my role as an insurance investigator with the possible exception of the chief of police. I fear that he may have already called Boston and discovered that my insurance company and I are a figment of your imagination, sir."

I thought for a minute and said, "No harm done, Franklin. We won't have to use the insurance thing again here in Amarillo."

Franklin went on to confirm what I had expected. He told us that the official line was Max and Jim Ed Leland are good old boys who had been in a few legal scrapes, but nothing serious. Franklin explained that the locals had gotten the same word that the Feds had received about laying off of these upstanding members of the community. The only thing that the sheriff or the chief of police had told Franklin about Lone Star Aviation was that it was a formerly great company that John Ivers had mismanaged, and John and Becky were fortunate that the Lelands had shown up to bail them out of their financial troubles.

Franklin went on to report, "I asked the chief of police his thoughts about the overly-heavy security around the King Jet hangar at the airport. I fear that he began suspecting my veracity at that point. The chief of police felt that the King Jet, being Lone Star's most significant asset, certainly warranted security precautions, and he was annoyed that anyone, particularly an insurance investigator, would be concerned about too much security. That is when I took my leave."

As the room grew silent, I realized Franklin had completed his report, so I said, "Monica, your turn."

Monica efficiently reported, "Between the library, the newspaper archives, and a very cooperative, dirty old man at the City Records Department, I know a lot more than I really want to about Max and Jim Ed Leland. The brief story is that Max and Jim Ed grew up here in Amarillo. They are the only two children in their family. Max is two years older. They were both above-average athletes and below-average students. They graduated from Amarillo high school in 1968. They both somehow stayed out of the Vietnam War and did not appear in any official records or news reports until the middle '70s. From then until now, there have been a string of arrests and indictments, but no convictions. A lot of people around them seem to get hurt or disappear. Recently, they show up quite often pictured with politicians and mid-level celebrities.

"In the last three years, it seems they have been throwing around a lot of money, including some pretty heavy campaign contributions and donations to all the respectable charities. The new Performing Arts Theatre under construction here in Amarillo will be named Leland Hall.

"All in all, Jake, on the outside it appears we have two all-American boys that made good. On the inside, although no one can put their finger on it, I know they're rotten to the core."

I filled Monica and Franklin in on my conversations with Bob Arnold and let them know that, with anything short of an open-and-shut-case with a smoking gun for evidence and a bus-load of nuns as witnesses, we weren't going to get any official help or even protection.

The three of us sat in silence for a few moments thinking our own thoughts.

I officially called our brief meeting to a close by suggesting we all get ready to have dinner at one of the local establishments. Monica mentioned she had seen *a cute little place called Aunt Molly's Kitchen downtown by the courthouse.* I told her I thought that would be fine, but I did detect a dubious sniff from Franklin as he closed the connecting door to his room.

## CHAPTER 14

t six o'clock, according to my Braille watch, Monica tapped on the connecting door to my motel room and let me know she was ready for dinner. Actually, as I remember, the phrase was *Jake, I'm going to die if you don't feed me right now*. I knocked on the other connecting door for Franklin, and he entered immediately as if he had been waiting.

As we walked downstairs to the parking lot, I felt good to be out of the motel room for the first time since we had arrived. Franklin opened the door, and Monica and I slid into the back seat of our super-duper, four-wheel-drive sports utility vehicle. As I settled into the seat, I thought, *As nice as this is, it's a long way from the Rolls.*

As Franklin drove us downtown to Aunt Molly's Kitchen

and whatever culinary delights might await us there, Monica let me know about the thought and preparation she had put into her wardrobe for the evening. She said, "Jake, I want you to know tonight you will be seen about Amarillo with a stunning version of an understated, sophisticated rodeo queen. I have gray cowboy boots, black jeans just tight enough to be interesting without being uncomfortable, and a mauve silk blouse to set off the entire ensemble."

"Mauve?" I questioned.

Monica knows my feelings on the subject of mauve, taupe, teal, and a number of other colors that I can't remember or that were developed after I lost my sight. I remember red and blue and green, but these other colors are a mystery to me. In a good-natured way, Monica always goes out of her way to bring these colors into our lives.

Monica explained, "Jake, I had to wear mauve because it will give the right hint of casual elegance for dinner at Aunt Molly's Kitchen. But the black jeans and gray boots will fit right in for our nine o'clock rendezvous with Deke Sawyer at the Road Kill Lounge. So, you see, there really was no other option."

I shot back with an impatience we both knew I didn't feel, "Well, Miss Rodeo Queen, since the mauve was imperative to our success in this mission, I'll let it go this time."

Monica patted my hand and said in the tone that launched a thousand ships, "Thank you, Jacob."

Franklin located Aunt Molly's Kitchen on the first try, and we all entered. Monica was on my arm and as Franklin had held the door for us, he walked in behind us. As Franklin entered, I heard a barely discernible rumble which indicated he was retracting the earlier sniff with respect to Aunt Molly's

Kitchen, and he was now willing to give it the benefit of the doubt. We were seated at a comfortable table and handed menus.

I followed my usual ritual which involves immediately closing my menu and setting it aside, after which Monica glances at her menu and casually asks, "What do you feel like tonight, Jake?"

I answered, "Something authentic. Maybe Tex-Mex."

Monica responded, just as if I were reading the menu with her, by saying, "Well, the Smoked Chicken Quesadillas look good."

I thought for a second and decided, "Sounds good to me. I believe I'll have that."

Monica ordered the same thing, and Franklin requested a complex Mexican concoction which he ordered in what sounded like accent-free Spanish. Our waitress was duly impressed and left to get our dinners started.

Monica giggled and said to Franklin, "Handsome, I had no idea you had mastered that Don Juan routine."

A satisfied rumble emanated as Franklin replied, "A left-over relic from a by-gone era, my dear."

So as not to violate our unwritten rule about not discussing business during dinner, I thought I'd better hurry up and express what was on my mind. "There's something I need to get on the table here with both of you. You two mean more to me than I can express for reasons I don't need to get into right now. But as you know, we have a wonderful and totally unique personal and professional relationship going for us back in Tulsa. This thing we're involved in now is so far above the call of duty compared to anything we have ever done before, and this is not even for a client. This is just me trying to even up a debt I owe to an old friend. Something tells me this could get really dangerous, and I guess what I'm trying to say is that if either or both of you want to get out of this deal, I wouldn't think any less of you."

Monica replied indignantly, "Jacob Dyer, are you trying to get out of buying me dinner? Because if you are, I want you to know I've been turned down by better people than you. I believe I'll stay right where I am."

Franklin emitted the seldom-heard volcanic rumble and said, "Mr. Dyer, as you are well aware, I am in the permanent service of Mrs. Maude Henson as a result of a prior arrangement with the late Mr. Henson, my benefactor. Mrs. Henson, for whatever reason, has felt compelled to have me assigned in your service for the past several years, which may I add, I have found most rewarding. I see no reason why a gentleman's agreement of long-standing should be brought into question for fear of some barbaric ruffians. As I have already taken up residence in the Armadillo Lodge and have mastered the conveyance known as a sports utility vehicle, I intend to stay and see this matter to its conclusion."

Monica applauded and said, "I wish I'd said that."

Shortly after our dinner arrived—and it was quite pleasant—Franklin surprised Monica and me by requesting additional hot sauce, and we talked of great books, wonderful music, and special people we had each known.

At eight o'clock, according to my Braille watch, I suggested we head back to our motel so that Monica and I could be already established at a prime location in the Road Kill Lounge before Colonel Sawyer hopefully appeared.

Thirty minutes later, Monica and I were in a corner booth, ready for action. Monica had already filled me in on the Road Kill Lounge's decor which ran heavy to shag carpet and Naugahyde furniture. Monica said the waitresses wore some kind of spandex garment between a work-out suit and a cheerleading uniform. Overall, it was not a good visual image.

A waitress approached our table and said in a smoke-deepened voice, "My name is Mabel. What'll you have?"

After Monica established they had no champagne, white wine, or Merlot, we both ordered a draft beer. Mabel returned shortly, and we sipped our beer as we waited patiently.

From long practice in similar situations, Monica and I have established a routine of seeming to be in deep conversation while making small talk to kill time while Monica surveys the room. At a little after nine, Monica casually mentioned that Deke Sawyer had just walked into the bar. She let me know he had settled onto a bar stool about 20 feet away from us and had ordered a drink. We continued our meaningless chatter to keep up a front until he had finished his drink.

Monica asked, "Our place or his, Jake?"

I replied, "Ours, I think. Why don't you go reel him in?"

Monica slid out of the booth, and I could hear her approach the bar and say in an inviting but respectable tone, "Excuse me, sir. I was wondering if you would like to join us for a drink?"

Monica returned shortly, and she slid into the booth across from me with Sawyer next to her. He said in a gruff voice, "Good evening. I know she's Monica, and who might you be?"

I said, "I am Jacob Dyer," and held out my hand. We shook.

Deke Sawyer said, "My mother always taught me I should

introduce myself, but sir, something tells me you already know who I am."

I asked nonchalantly, "What makes you think that, Mr. Sawyer?"

He sighed and said, "Occasionally, in my past, someone out of the blue has offered to buy me a drink, but that has been very rare in recent years. But what is beyond rare is to have a young lady the caliber of this one ask to buy me a drink."

I laughed and said, "She is, indeed, of the highest caliber, but as you surmised, I know that you are Colonel Deke Sawyer, and we just wanted to ask you a few friendly questions."

Sawyer paused for a moment and replied, "Well, I guess if you're buying the drinks, I'll see if I can come up with some friendly answers."

Mabel asked if we wanted two more beers. When I nodded *Yes*, she left. I assumed that her background with Sawyer automatically told her he would want another drink and what kind of drink it would be.

I casually slid into my questions. "We'd like to know a little bit about Lone Star Aviation, and Larry at the bar told Monica that you've been there longer than anyone else."

"What would you like to know?" he asked guardedly.

I replied, "Oh, just background stuff. How you came to Lone Star, what you think of it, that sort of thing."

Colonel Deke Sawyer paused and then told us that he had spent 20 years in the military and retired when it became apparent that the rank of Colonel was as high as he was destined to rise. He took his 20-year retirement pay and looked for civilian work, but couldn't think of a life without flying. Then he ran into Charlie Owens who was the flamboyant founder and president of Lone Star Aviation. The company was at a

THE SOUND OF HONOR

high point, and Sawyer was proud to become a pilot on an elite team.

Then Sawyer got a bit of a pained tone in his voice and said, "I haven't always been a second-rate flyer in a third-rate outfit. Sometimes things just end up that way. But, lovely lady and mysterious gentleman, drink or no drink, without some real square answers from you, you've just got your last answer out of me."

When you're trying to unravel a mystery, it's hard to know where to start. There are times when the best thing to do is simply find a loose thread, pull it, and hope for the best. Since we didn't have a whole lot of other threads to pull on, I decided we would have to trust Deke Sawyer.

olonel Deke Sawyer was one of those people who do not feel uncomfortable with silence. He was prepared to sit there as long as it took to get the answers he wanted, and I knew that—as in the staring contests we used to have when we were kids—this guy simply wouldn't blink. So, I broke the silence.

"Colonel Sawyer, I'm going to level with you and trust you."

Sawyer shot back, "Why would you trust me?"

I replied, "Because I knew Charlie Owens. I didn't know him well, but I knew him as the father-in-law of my best friend. And if Charlie Owens trusted you, you're good enough for me."

Sawyer's tone warmed slightly. "I appreciate that, and I will try to live up to your faith in Charlie and Charlie's faith in me."

I filled Sawyer in on my visit from Becky and everything we had discovered since. I concluded by saying, "The bottom line is, Colonel Sawyer, Max and Jim Ed Leland robbed my best friend, ruined his reputation and that of Lone Star Aviation, and when John found out what kind of operation they were running, I believe they killed him."

There was another long silence, and I knew Deke Sawyer wasn't going to be rushed, so I waited him out. Finally, he spoke. "For now, I'm going to take you at face value and assume you may know what you're talking about. I know there's a lot of things that aren't right at Lone Star. I just can't put my finger on them. I fly a broken down old crate that barely passes inspection. Three days a week, I ferry cargo to Dallas, pick up a load, and come back. Most of the rest of my time is spent either here or in my shabby apartment near the airport. But I know there's something going on with the King Jet that only a few people are in on."

He sighed and continued, "Sometimes, folks, we don't know what's going on because we don't want to look too deeply for fear of what we might find."

Sawyer lapsed into one of his long pauses and then said in a tone reminiscent of a Colonel, "Let me make one thing very clear to both of you. I work for Lone Star Aviation. That doesn't mean much now, but it used to mean everything. And one of the things I learned early on from Charlie Owens—if you take a man's money, you do his work. The old timers here in Texas call it *riding for the brand*. It means you're on the team, no matter how tough it gets, but if Max and Jim Ed are mixed up in something illegal and they did what you said to John Ivers, I will do what I can to stop it."

We knew where he stood. He wasn't totally on our side, but I knew that if we were right about what was going on with Lone Star Aviation, we could count on Deke Sawyer to do what he felt was honorable.

I thought for a moment and asked, "Colonel Sawyer, assuming for a moment that Lone Star's King Jet is running drugs or illegal aliens, how do we prove it? It seems like the only thing they do with the jet is take brief training runs every-other day."

Deke laughed bitterly and said, "I don't know what they're doing, but they're not taking training runs. First off, there's no one to train because Lone Star is cutting every pilot they have. Secondly, if they were going to train somebody, why would they train them in a jet like that if they're going to fly a crate like mine?"

He took another one of his familiar pauses and said in a low tone, "You're going to have to watch very closely what they're doing with that jet, but I want to warn you, if you get too close, someone will get hurt—or maybe worse. It's happened before. The only direction I can give you is that if they're taking training flights every other day, somewhere they have to file a flight plan, fill out logs, and keep fuel records. Those will tell the story."

I thanked Deke Sawyer for his time and asked him if we could call him when we got some more information to go on.

He said, "I will stand by what I said. If there's something wrong at Lone Star, I want to try to make it right. But don't forget who I work for. If you get some details that you want to run by a broken-down old flyer, just contact your friend,

Larry, at the bar. He generally knows where to find me."

He stood up but did not move away from our table. He said, "Ma'am, it's been a pure pleasure to meet you, and sir, when this is all over, I'll buy you a drink, and you can tell me why this means so much to you."

I heard his footsteps as he walked away.

Monica and I sat for a long time and wrestled with a plan to somehow reach into the tiger's cage for the information we needed without getting our proverbial hand bitten completely off.

#. #. #.

I heard John say for what must have been the tenth time, "Okie, it's about time for you to get back in the game. The whole world's been moving on, and you and I have been running around in circles on the beach here in California. It's time for us to catch up."

I shared with John my feelings of fear and inadequacy. I tried to explain that I knew we had come a long way, but I wasn't ready to go home and face my friends and family. Thoughts of a looming career and a young lady left behind long ago were inconceivable to me.

John said, "If we wait 'til we feel ready or feel comfortable, I'm afraid we'll die right here."

John always used the word *we* when referring to me and my problems, but over the past several months, he had earned that right.

I agreed to give it my best shot with a lot more confidence than I felt. We checked out of the rehab center, and Sharon—who I had dubbed Attila the Hun—turned into an emotional tower of Jello as she cried through the entire going-away party she had arranged for me. Coincidentally, John's shattered leg was instantly 100% recovered the day I was ready to leave.

I thanked everyone in the rehab center for everything they had done and tried to do for me. John and I left the rehab center in a taxi and headed for the airport. As we were riding across the LA basin to catch a jet that would eventually take me back to everything I had left in Tulsa a million years ago—before Vietnam, before the helicopter explosion, before the hospital ship, before the rehab center—I kept hearing the line from the *Wizard of Oz* playing over and over in my head: *There's no place like home.* But I knew I wasn't going home to the place I left. I knew I would have to find a new way to relate to the people and the places I had known before.

Through the endless hours on the hospital ship and in rehab, I had carried another memory from *The Wizard of Oz* which was the magical moment that everything went from black and white to color. I had somehow imagined that if I could get home, everything would be the way it was before, and I would instantly go from darkness to light just like in the movie when Dorothy arrived in Oz.

But as the taxi let us out at Los Angeles International Airport, I knew I had been kidding myself. I knew that dark was dark whether you were in the jungles of Vietnam, a hospital ship, a beach on the Pacific Ocean, or where you grew up in Tulsa, Oklahoma. You can run, but you can't hide.

As I held John's elbow with one hand and my cane with the other, we made our way through the immense airport toward our gate. I found myself dreading everything before me, and I walked slower and slower. John sensed my hesitant pace which I believe he intuitively knew corresponded to the winding down in my spirit.

He paused and said, "Okie, let's stop here for a second. This leg is just killing me. You know, I didn't want to leave rehab, because I know I still have a long way to go before this thing gets back the way it should. But I figured sometimes you just gotta go ahead and do what you gotta do. It's like jumping into a cold lake or pulling off a Band-Aid. The best way to do it is just to get it over with. So I figured it was time for me to get out of there and try to get back into the real world somehow, and I really appreciate you being here with me. It's not easy to do all by yourself."

I knew instantly what a farce John's words were. Two statements leaped into my mind to shout out at John. One was *You are a liar.* The other was *I love you.* I kept both statements inside me as we walked to the plane.

The boarding area was a zoo. People were milling about, impatiently waiting for departure time. The ticket agent checked our boarding passes and then said to John, "We allow pre-boarding for disabled people."

John laughed and said, "Ma'am, I really appreciate that. This leg got shot up, and we had a bit of a hard landing. Sometimes it just doesn't want to cooperate, and if I can get on the plane a little early, it would be easier. By the way, he's with me."

John and I moved down the jetway and onto the plane. He found our seats, and we settled in. I fought back a wave of panic and disorientation as I realized I didn't know where I was or where I was going, and the world instantly closed in on me.

As always, John sensed my anxiety and recounted the exploits of his Uncle Delbert's fishing trip and everything that had gone wrong. It was such a ridiculous story, and it was so incongruous with the terror that was squeezing me tighter and tighter. John went on with his slapstick story, and just when I was preparing to ask him why in the world he thought I might remotely care about his Uncle Delbert's stupid fishing trip, I realized we were already in the air and leveling off toward Dallas where we would catch the connecting flight to Tulsa.

As we flew over Arizona 30,000 feet below, I thought about John who was pretending to be dozing next to me. I thought about how many times I had wanted to give up on myself and would have easily done so except for the fact that I would have let him down.

# # #

I did my best not to let him down then, and I didn't want to let him down as Monica and I walked upstairs to our motel rooms.

Monica asked, "You got the plan yet, boss?"

"Not yet," I replied.

She said confidently, "Well, you'll have the plan in the morning, and I know it'll be the right one. It always is."

As we each closed our motel room doors, I said to myself *Dyer, you'd better have the right plan this time, because if you don't, I don't think you're going to get a second chance.*

CHAPTER 16

ack in my room, I sat on the bed, dialed the motel operator, and asked for room service. I ordered a pot of hot coffee and one cup. It was going to be a long night.

There are certain tasks in life that seem so intimidating that we become frozen in our inactivity. You can fool yourself a while by doing preliminary things or talking about the task at hand, but there comes a point when everything—with respect to preparation—that can be done has been completed, and it's time to quit talking about it and get started. My problem was I didn't know exactly where to start, and I felt like someone walking through a mine field. You really want to get it right the first time.

I lit one of my Mexican cigars and leaned back on the bed to let my thoughts wash over me. I was hoping that their random pattern would somehow fall into enough order to at least point the way to start.

A knock sounded at my door. I opened it and smelled freshly brewed coffee. A young man said, "Good evening, sir. I'll just place this here on the table."

I held out my hand, and the waiter gave me a bill and a pen. I scribbled my name somewhere near what I hoped was the bottom of the check. I handed him back the paperwork and pen and reached into my pocket where I had two crumpled bills. I gave him what I knew was either a five dollar bill or a twenty dollar bill. He said most excitedly, "Thank you very much, sir!" Whether it was the five or the twenty, he seemed very pleased as he left my room and closed the door.

I poured a cup of coffee and sat in one of the chairs smoking my cigar and sipping the surprisingly good coffee.

#. #. #.

Airline coffee is notoriously bad. This is made even worse by the fact that the flight attendants are seldom able to get the coffee hot enough for my taste. I was drinking a lukewarm, weak cup of coffee as I heard the pilot say over the intercom, "Ladies and gentlemen, we'll be landing in Tulsa in approximately twelve minutes. We hope you've enjoyed our flight and the next time you make travel plans you'll think of us."

John had told me that he had made a few phone calls, and my parents and a handful of friends and family members would be on hand to greet us. He had been tentative when he told me, "Your mother assured me everyone was looking forward to seeing you, and they would bring Mary Ann to the airport."

I had tried not to think about Mary Ann during the time on the hospital ship and in rehab. I never really expected to get through the ordeal, so the thought of coming home and confronting her and all of the questions left behind really never concerned me.

Mary Ann and I had met in junior high school, and we had been a couple all through high school. We had gone to dances and said all the right things that we believed young people trying to be adults are supposed to say. Although it had never been specifically discussed, we both assumed we would continue our predictable pattern and get married when I returned from Vietnam. As I looked back on it, our relationship would be better defined as comfortable and predictable rather than loving or passionate.

I knew that all of the anxiety and fear of the unknown I was feeling was also being felt by my friends, family, and—most particularly—Mary Ann. I knew she would feel trapped by some unspoken promise from long ago. Even if I still had my eyes, I knew I was a different person than the boy who had left Oklahoma 14 months earlier.

For Mary Ann, the 14 months were little more than a year of junior college and a summer working at the mall. We had exchanged the minimally-expected number of letters. Those letters had featured small talk more than dealing with the real unspoken questions.

As I heard the landing gear of our jet being lowered, I began to feel the panic closing in on me again. This wasn't just the normal panic I felt from being forced to live in darkness without the tools to cope with it. This was a panic born from realizing that, without meaning to, I had dragged my friends, family, and even Mary Ann into the darkness with me.

There is no sensation or emotion that only touches one person. We are all like separate nerve endings within the same organism. For the first time, I realized that my suffering had caused pain and was going to cause more pain to those I cared about.

With my new realization of shared pain, I felt that I had to say something to John for everything he had gone through with me. I nudged John in the seat next to me. I heard him yawn and stretch. He said, "Well, Okie, down there is home sweet Oklahoma. It won't be long now."

I said, "John, I need you to know that I realize you've been through this pain and torture with me, and that deserves more thanks than I can express. I had no choice in whether or not to deal with this, but you did; and I realize that has cost you."

John paused for a few moments and replied, "Okie, the pain of going through this with you is not near as bad as the pain I would have felt had I not been here knowing you were going through this alone. As bad as it has been, it's been easier for me to be a part of it."

#. #. #.

As I sat in my motel room trying to formulate a plan, for the first time I really understood John's feelings from long ago. As much as I hated what had happened to Lone Star and John and Becky, the pain was somehow soothed by being here and doing what I could to try to make it right.

As I tapped the last ash from my cigar and drained my coffee cup, I laid back on the bed. As I let my mind drift toward sleep, the first subtleties of a plan appeared in the distant corner of my mind.

I slept the sleep of innocent children, righteous adults, and those who have undertaken tasks far beyond their abilities and comprehension. The telephone woke me. I fumbled and caught it on the second ring.

Monica said, "Mr. Dyer, this is your 8 a.m. wake-up call. It's a lovely day in Amarillo. The humidity is already a swampy ninety two per cent, and our temperature today is expected to climb beyond the century mark. Weather suitable for steaming rice and vegetables.

"Franklin and I are heading for the mandatory caffeine and blessed bagels, and I felt you might want this call so that you could get yourself situated before we return. The entire management and staff of the Armadillo Lodge wish you a pleasant day."

She hung up the phone without allowing me to utter so much as a *Good morning*.

I showered, dressed, and prepared for the day. I was just putting the final touches on my hair—which is not easy in the dark—and hoping I wasn't having a bad-hair-day when I heard the knock on my door. I opened the door to the familiar and welcomed first rumble of the morning.

Franklin greeted me, "Good morning, sir. Another hot one, I'm afraid. I'll just spread our breakfast fare here on the table."

Franklin and I resumed our seats from the day before, and the princess took her seat on the corner of my bed. Monica said in a cheerful voice that let me know she had already been into the coffee, "Good morning, Jake. I'm glad you're up."

I replied, "Some nasty old lady here at the motel called me at eight o'clock and woke me up. She had the most disgusting voice and disagreeable personality you could imagine."

Franklin emitted a brief sniff and replied, "Most frightening, sir."

I then felt a wadded-up bagel wrapper bounce off my chest. Monica said pleasantly, "If you don't watch yourself, my next shot will be a cup of coffee."

Considering Monica's history in such matters and my clean shirt, I determined to remain silent. We each set about eating our breakfast, and I knew that Monica and Franklin were waiting on me.

As I finished my last bite of bagel, I began, "Here's the deal. We have got to find out what's going on with that King Jet, because it's the key to everything. Franklin, I would like you to take Monica to an upscale video store, and purchase a camera suitable for surveillance as well as our old TV reporter routine."

Surprisingly, I heard a very low rumble which is highly irregular as Franklin is never one to interrupt. He said, "Excuse me, but if I may, sir. After conversing with Miss Monica before we left Tulsa, I took the liberty of packing our camera and equipment, anticipating just such an eventuality."

I chuckled, "Franklin, you are the best. Remind me to tell Miss Maude to give you a raise."

Franklin emitted a satisfied rumble and said, "That won't be necessary, sir."

I explained that since the King Jet hangar seemed to have a lot of security around it, we needed the camera situated so we could monitor who went in and out and what was going on around the clock. Franklin suggested that the Lone Star hangar—which housed all of their older equipment—was next door, and there might be a way to situate a camera in that building to monitor the King Jet hangar. I asked Franklin if he had any suggestions since he had been in the building during his fact-finding tour through the airport.

He said, "Sir, as I remember, that hangar has an office on the second level at the far end of the building which would be facing the King Jet hangar. There were stairs leading up to the office from inside the hangar, and I believe there would have to be some attic space above that office."

Monica sounded concerned. "Frankie, how in the world are you going to get up there?"

Franklin replied coolly, "Well, miss, with the poorly-maintained state of their aircraft, I cannot imagine that the filters in their heater and air conditioning units have been changed recently. I suggest that a representative from Franklin's Heat and Air could get into that attic with very little difficulty."

I told Franklin to be careful and be sure to put in a long-play tape. I reminded him to situate the camera somewhere so that we could get the tape back later and put in a fresh one if needed. Franklin replied confidently, "Very good, sir. Consider it done."

"Monica," I began, "the fuel records may be the key to everything. We need to find out when they fuel that jet and how much they are burning. I suggest that you, my dear, are a representative of the Texas Energy Commission. You have been assigned to the Fuel Tax Task Force. It seems that some airport operators have not been submitting all of their tax revenues that they collect when customers purchase fuel. As a diligent public servant, you are reviewing records of fuel purchases to make sure that the appropriate tax revenue has been paid."

Monica replied in a convincing West Texas accent, "We have all been real concerned about the fuel tax shortfall, and with a routine review of the fuel records, I'm sure we can clear this matter up faster than you can say Sam Houston."

As Franklin and Monica left the motel for their individual tasks, I wondered for the thousandth time what I had done to deserve the loyalty of two such multi-talented people as Monica and Franklin. I knew it would take every bit of talent they possessed and every bit of luck we could get to save Becky Ivers and Lone Star Aviation without ending up in a lonely grave like John Ivers.

CHAPTER 17

s the jet jolted onto the runway at Tulsa International Airport, I realized I was back in Tulsa, but I wasn't home. The people waiting to greet the Jacob Dyer who had left here 14 months ago would be meeting me for the first time. I realized that since the helicopter had exploded and the world had gone dark, nothing had been fair. It wasn't fair to me, it wasn't fair to John, and now I was getting ready to expose my friends, my family, and Mary Ann to this inequity of darkness.

As the jet rumbled across the tarmac, John sensed my mounting anxiety. He asked, "How are you doing, Okie?"

I shot back in an anger not intended for John, "How do you think I'm doing? I'm getting ready to tarnish everyone I care about with this terrible thing, and it's not fair to expect them to be able to deal with this. And what about Mary Ann?

Maybe we didn't have it together real well, but we cared about one another and, eventually, we would have gotten married. Now she's caught in this terrible trap that she can't get out of. I just don't want to make all these people join me in this thing."

John replied calmly, "Okie, do you know what your problem is? Your problem is that you underestimate who you are and the people who are in your life. You are a formidable personality, and I know that everyone we're going to meet here has been impacted by you in some way. You've got to give these people some credit, and you've also got to give them the benefit of the doubt. You and I have had a long time to adjust to this thing. These people know about it, but they haven't experienced it. Give them a little time and space, and I think you'll be impressed."

As the plane stopped at the gate, I asked frantically, "What do I say to Mary Ann? Do I let her off the hook? Do I tell her to forget the whole thing? Do we start over?"

As John and I stood up, and we both moved down the aisle, he said, "Okie, when in doubt, tell the truth. If you and Mary Ann thought enough of each other to be serious, at least think enough of her to tell her how you feel, and you both will figure this out together."

As we stepped into the jet bridge tunnel that would lead us to the terminal, I felt depressed and said, "John, I can't imagine why anyone would want to be involved in any kind of a relationship with me."

I felt John's arm around my shoulder, and he laughed and said, "For a guy who spent the last year with you and has been with you day and night since the hospital ship, I find that a little insulting."

"Look, I didn't mean you. I'm sorry."

John said, "Listen, Okie, there's no chains attaching me to you or you to me. I'm here because I want to be, but there is one small favor you can do for me. This suitcase is getting a little heavy for my battered old leg. If you could fold up that white cane, we could slip it in the outside pocket of the suitcase, and we could each hold the handle as we walk out together. That would sure take a lot of pressure off my leg."

As we walked the few steps remaining to the terminal—just as John had arranged it, so that my friends and family as well as Mary Ann would see John and me walk out together without a white cane in evidence—I said, "John, I don't know what to say."

He replied, "I've been trying to tell you all along. Sometimes, you just gotta do the right thing. And maybe someday, Okie, you'll do something for me."

#. #. #.

My motel room was feeling very small. With Monica and Franklin gone, my umbilical cord had effectively been cut. I didn't want to think about it, and I didn't want to think about Monica and Franklin being in danger.

I put a Mozart CD on the portable stereo and tried to mentally examine all the angles. In even the most complex situation, there is usually one factor upon which everything hinges. Complicated problems are simple once you locate the key element. The common denominators are generally the predictable, human frailties. As I was pondering this, the phone rang.

I said, "Hello," and heard Monica say, "Jake, this is your talented, intelligent, and gorgeous associate."

I laughed and said, "How are you, Franklin?"

Monica said, "Jake, if you knew what a good job I have done, you'd be a little more respectful."

I replied, "Sorry. What did you find out?"

Monica adopted her efficient tone and said, "Jake, there are three separate places to buy fuel here at the Amarillo Airport. The King Jet leaves every other day for a several-hour training run and returns here, but they never buy fuel. This plane is fueled up somewhere else during these training runs."

I was shocked and asked, "Are you sure?"

Monica replied in her Texas drawl, "Why, Jacob Dyer, no upstanding Texan would lie to a duly authorized member of the Texas Energy Commission."

I told Monica to wait at the airport until Franklin had set up the video equipment to spy on the King Air hangar. She told me they would return together as soon as Franklin was done. As I hung up the phone, I was more confused than ever, but I knew we were on the right track.

I then dialed the number I had memorized for Lone Star Aviation. After the young lady greeted me by saying, *Good afternoon, this is Lone Star Aviation. May I help you?*, I explained to her that I was with Customer Service at the King Jet Aviation Corporation, and we were correlating some in-flight data records to determine fuel efficiency on our late-model jets. I asked if she could get me the name of the contractor that supplied fuel for Lone Star Aviation's King Jet.

She seemed bewildered and a bit flustered and asked, "Are you calling from Harlingen?"

I replied with the only answer that I knew would keep the conversation going, "Yes, ma'am. I'm right here in Harlingen."

She replied, "Well, all the records should be there, because that's the only place that we have ever bought fuel for the King Jet. May I ask again who this is and what your interest is in our fuel?"

I hung up. After a brief call to the library, I discovered that Harlingen, Texas is near the Mexican border and is over 750 miles from Amarillo. There is only one airport that takes commercial jets, so I knew we were getting closer to unraveling whatever it was that was going on with Lone Star.

After a few more minutes, I had gotten the number of the Harlingen field from Directory Assistance, and I dialed the number for the control tower. I heard an official-sounding voice say, "Harlingen Tower. May I help you?"

I explained, "Sir, my name is Roland Hicks. I am with Lone Star Aviation. We seem to have some discrepancies in our records relating to some of our training flights that have refueled at your airport. I was hoping you could direct me to someone who could help me fill in the blanks in our records."

He answered sternly, "Listen, Hicks, I don't know what you people are doing, but they're not training runs. And your little games circling back and forth over our airport got one of my best controllers fired."

I asked, "What are you talking about?"

His tone changed, and he sounded very guarded when he asked, "What was your name again, and why can't you check the flight plans on your end?"

I hung up the phone.

I dialed the same number again, and using my bored bureaucrat voice, I asked, "Can you connect me with your Personnel Director, please?"

I was put on hold, and another extension rang. It was answered by a cheerful young lady who said, "This is Marlene.

May I help you?"

I replied, "Yes, ma'am. This is Reggie Fields at the Texas Employment Security Commission. We've had a claim for unemployment insurance from one of your air traffic controllers, but this file is all messed up. I thought instead of sending it back down there and holding up the claim for a few more months, I would try to clear this up on the phone."

She said, "Sir, the only air traffic controller who's left has been Billy Spears."

I replied as if confirming my own records, "Yes, ma'am, my records show that would be a William Spears. My records don't show a reason for dismissal or a current phone number. I'm hoping you could look that up for me."

She said, "The phone number is simple."

As she read it off to me, I committed it to memory. "And the reason for dismissal?" I asked.

She replied, "Well, I don't have to look that up. Everyone knows Billy Spears was fired for drinking on the job. He nearly ran a commercial airliner into some training flight from one of the charter services."

I replied, "Ma'am, this seems to complete my form, and I appreciate your help. This will enable us to get Mr. Spears' claim in the works immediately."

She told me good-bye, and we both hung up.

Sometimes, with nothing to show for it and no evidence to support you, everything just clicks in your head, and you know you're on the right track. It's as easy as peeling away the layers to reveal what's underneath.

I said to myself aloud, "Dyer, just remember that under one of those layers, there's a snake ready, willing, and able to bite you."

I dialed the number I had memorized for Billy Spears. It rang a number of times, and just as I was preparing to hang up, a sleepy, young female voice said, "Yeah."

I asked, "Is Billy there?"

She laughed bitterly and said, "Billy ain't never here, and when he is, he sure isn't in any shape to talk on the phone."

"Well, can you tell me where I might find him?" I asked.

She said, "Your best bet, and really your only bet, is to find him at the Cockpit Lounge, hangin' around with all those flyers and airport people."

She hung up without allowing me to thank her, and as I was considering everything I had learned, Franklin and Monica returned.

Franklin seemed very pleased with himself as he told me, "Sir, the camera is installed and functioning, and on extra-slow speed, we will get 24 hours of delayed video."

"Did you have any problems getting in?" I asked.

Franklin rumbled briefly and replied, "No, sir. I met one gentleman who was in the upper office on the phone. I believe he was placing a wager on a horse race. I told him about the air filter, and he simply waved me down the hall where I found a ladder into the attic area where I set up the camera. We have a beautiful view of the King Jet hangar and the surrounding area through an air vent. When the door opens, we'll be able to see inside. If Lone Star stays to their every-other-day schedule, we should capture their departure on video early tomorrow morning."

"Do you think we'll have any trouble getting back in to retrieve the video?" I asked.

Franklin sniffed a bit indignantly and replied, "No, sir. I told the sporting gentleman who had directed me down the hall that it was an odd-sized filter, and I would have to come back tomorrow. I have taken the liberty of purchasing the appropriate filter which I will, indeed, replace tomorrow as the original is in a horrendous state."

"Very nice, handsome," Monica purred.

A satisfied rumble was forthcoming.

I filled Monica and Franklin in on each of my calls, and we had a brief discussion about what we knew and where we should go from here. It seemed that the thread we were pulling led us to an unemployed air traffic controller in South Texas named Billy Spears.

CHAPTER 18

The next morning, Monica, Franklin, and I went to breakfast at our one and only favorite restaurant in Amarillo, Aunt Molly's Kitchen. Franklin ordered coffee and dry toast, I had oatmeal with my coffee, and Monica ordered one of everything on the menu.

I laughed as I asked, "How can you do that and still stop traffic with your youthful figure?"

Monica replied, "The key is my addiction to my Stairmaster. If I didn't exercise and kept eating like this, I would still be able to stop traffic, but it would be because I was blocking the intersection."

Our unwritten rules are adamant regarding talking about business at dinner, but the rules are somewhat vague regarding breakfast or lunch. So, after we had finished eating and were on our second cups of coffee, I said, "Franklin, I think it would be best if you replace the air filter later this morning and switch tapes. Monica and I are going to catch a connecting flight through Dallas to Harlingen and try to have a visit with Billy Spears. With any luck, we should be back tonight for dinner, and if you could arrange to have a VCR in my room, we can review the tape of the King Jet hangar."

Franklin replied, "Very good, sir."

Franklin dropped Monica and me off at the airport terminal which was on the opposite end of the airport complex from Lone Star Aviation. We consulted the flights through Dallas to Harlingen and realized we had fourteen minutes to catch a flight that would have us there early in the afternoon.

Monica and I hurriedly walked to the gate where the agent made us a return reservation that would have us back in Amarillo at 8 p.m. We had already decided that Franklin would pick us up outside the terminal that evening unless we left him a message to the contrary at the motel. Monica took my arm, and we boarded the plane just as they were closing the door.

As we slipped into our first-class seats, Monica said, "It's a good thing Amarillo has a small airport like Tulsa, or we wouldn't have made it."

As our plane lifted off the runway for the short connecting flight to Dallas/Ft. Worth, I thought about the Tulsa International Airport. While I agreed with Monica that it was easy to get in and out of in a hurry, I remember the longest walk of my life through that airport with John Ivers over 25 years before.

#. #. #.

As John and I walked through the glass door into the terminal, we were both clutching the handle of his suitcase. I knew that it wasn't that heavy, and his leg was fine, but entering the airport in this fashion allowed me to walk in without holding the white cane which, at that time, I still thought of as a mark of shame.

I could hear a number of people milling about, and I heard a few voices say, "There he is," and one voice in a surprised tone say, "He looks okay to me."

My mother and father called to me and rushed over. My father gave me his typical bear hug, and my mother kissed me on the cheek. I could tell that she was crying. I introduced John to them, and my mother asked me, "Jacob, why wouldn't you let us come and see you in the rehab hospital in California?"

As I was trying to formulate a way to explain to this dear woman, without hurting her, all of my thoughts and feelings that surrounded needing to be alone during rehab, I heard John say, "Mr. and Mrs. Dyer, I can't tell you how many times Jacob told me that he wanted to fly both of you out there to be with him. But the military rehab hospital has a very strict policy. And you know how that red tape can be."

This seemed to satisfy my parents and got me off the hook. John carried most of the conversation as he was introduced to a number of relatives and friends of the family. My mother came close to me and said, "Jacob, Mary Ann's here."

I heard Mary Ann's distantly familiar voice say, "Hi Jake. How are you feeling?"

"Okay," was all I could manage to reply.

We hugged like cousins in church and stood there awkwardly. John said, "Well, Jake, all the wonderful things you told me about Mary Ann certainly seem to be true, and I'm looking forward to getting to know everyone a lot better. But, Jake, this leg, as you know, is still acting up, and if you can help me with my bag, I think I can make it to the parking lot."

John and I got into the back seat of my parents' car, and in a few minutes, we were pulling into the driveway of the home where I had grown up and where I had left 14 months and a lifetime earlier.

My mother said, "John, I hope both you and Jacob will be comfortable in his old room. There are two twin beds, and I hope you'll have enough room for your things."

My father boomed out, "Mother, these boys have been in the Army. This will be the best quarters they've had since they left home."

My mother expressed her concern. "John will you be able to make it up the stairs all right?"

John replied, "Ma'am that'll be just what the doctor ordered, because I'm supposed to exercise this leg, and stairs are just the thing."

John and I walked into the house together, and it was like being in a familiar place but everything was somehow different. I knew vaguely where things were, but the pictures in my head did not always correspond to the things I heard, smelled, and felt.

As John and I navigated up the stairs and into my old room, I lay back on the familiar bed and realized I had come home to a place I had never been before. And I was a stranger in a strange land.

My mother came upstairs and told me that the church was hosting a welcome home dinner for John and me that night. She said it would be over early, and then a few relatives, close friends, and Mary Ann would be coming back to the house for dessert. My mother seemed to work a questioning tone into the statement, "We know you'll want to spend some time alone with Mary Ann."

My mother went back downstairs, explaining she had some last minute details to work out in preparation for the dinner. John and I lay on the twin beds, lost in our own thoughts. Finally, John said, "Jake, these are some really great people. You are lucky to have a family like this. The only family I'll ever have is the one I'll inherit if I can catch Becky Owens at a weak moment and get her to marry me."

I replied, "I know they're great people, but do you realize no one has mentioned *the B word*? They ask about your leg, but no one has said anything about me being blind. It's like it's a dirty word."

I could hear John blow out a long stream of air, and he said, "Okie, I told you to give them a chance. They don't know what to say, and they're afraid they'll make a mistake. It'll work out."

I didn't feel comfortable in my parents' home, and then I realized that it was the most familiar place in my world. It was my home, and if I didn't feel normal there, I wondered if I could ever feel normal again.

#. #. #.

With Monica on my arm to guide me, we made it through the maze known as Dallas/Ft. Worth International Airport and caught our connecting flight. Our plane into Harlingen was on-time. As we had no luggage, we walked directly out of the airport and caught a cab.

Our driver, an elderly gentleman with a bit of a military tone, asked, "Where to, sir?"

I replied, "The Cockpit Lounge."

After a bit of an uncomfortable silence, he replied, "It's very close to the airport here, sir, but are you sure that's where you want to go?"

I replied, "Yes, I'm sure, and on the way there, you can tell me why you question the fact that that's where we want to go."

He said, "Sir, it's my job to take people anywhere they want, and that's what I'll do. I just didn't think that a gentleman like you and certainly a lady like her would be interested in the Cockpit Lounge."

I explained that we were not really interested in the Lounge, itself, but one of its regular patrons. When I mentioned the name Billy Spears, our driver said, "A sad case, that one."

I said, "Tell us about it."

Our driver said, "Billy got fired for drinking on the job. Billy is one of those guys that drank a lot but always took his job seriously. He knew how to manage his drinking, if you know what I mean. They say he made a mistake because he was drunk. I don't believe it. Now, since he got fired, he has slid completely off the wagon. There's no reason for Billy to manage his drinking, because that airport job meant everything to him. And now, he's got nothing left but a few friends, a lot of old memories, and a liquor bottle."

We pulled to a stop, and our driver said, "Here you are, sir—the Cockpit Lounge, such as it is." He said, "That'll be $5.40 on the meter, sir."

I reached into my pocket and pulled out five twenty-dollar bills I had folded at the corners the way I always fold twenty dollar bills when I remember to do it properly. I handed him the one hundred dollars and asked, "Can you wait here while we have a conversation with Mr. Spears?"

He replied in a very pleased tone, "Sir, this will hold me right here until about Thursday."

Monica and I stepped out of the cab, and as she took my arm, she described the Cockpit Lounge. She said, "Here we are again. Top drawer all the way, Jake. This is a cinder block building, painted bright orange, with a purple hand-painted sign. It looks like it used to be a gas station or something. The cab we arrived in is ten years old and is the best-looking vehicle in the parking lot."

We opened the screen door which creaked on its hinges and entered the Cockpit Lounge. Monica said so only I would hear, "Concrete floor, metal chairs, exposed light bulbs, a couple of mis-matched booths, and an ancient pool table. Our host at the bar could be cast as a serial killer if he ever decides to go into the movies. All in all, Jake, it's got atmosphere."

A gravelly voice from the bar said, "Is there something I can do for you folks?"

Monica and I walked toward the voice, and I said, "We're looking for Billy Spears."

The bartender asked, "Why do you want Billy? Are you reporters?"

I replied, "No, we're not reporters. We do want to ask him some questions about his job, though. We think he got a raw deal, and we'd like to help him."

I pulled one of the folded twenties out of my pocket and extended it toward the voice. He snatched the twenty from my hand and responded, "You'll find Billy at the last table on the left."

As Monica and I walked down the length of the bar, she covertly said, "This guy could be the poster child for Alcoholics Anonymous. He has really seen better days. I hope we can help him."

Each time Dyer Straits Lost and Found undertakes to find something that someone has lost or had taken from them, in addition to making money and doing our job, we try to help anyone who has been hurt along the way. I think it's a bit of the Don Quixote complex in me. We are the champion of lost causes.

As we sat down at the rickety table with Billy Spears, I knew he was a lost cause, and I hoped we could help him. I also hoped he could help us. As I mentally took measure of our situations, it was hard to determine who was in worse shape—Billy Spears or Jacob Dyer.

CHAPTER 19

Before I could say anything, the voice I came to know as belonging to Billy Spears croaked, "What do you two want?"

I replied, "My name's Jacob Dyer and this is Monica Stone, and believe it or not, we would like to help you and have you help us."

Billy Spears responded, "You can just go back to wherever you came from, because after what I've been through, I know there isn't anyone who's going to help me."

Seldom does Monica enter into a conversation I'm having when I'm working, but on rare occasions, she jumps in at the right place and at the right time to turn the tide for us. I knew this was just such an occasion when I heard Monica say, "Billy Spears, look directly into my baby blue eyes so that you'll know

I'm not kidding when I tell you that this man sitting here next to me is the only chance you've got in the world of recovering your job, your self-respect, and your life. And if you don't get your attitude straight in about the next two minutes, he and I are going to walk out of here and leave you in this pigsty. Now, he will get us where we're going 'cause he always does, but friend, this is your last chance, and I suggest you take it right now."

There was a long pause as I mentally gave Monica a standing ovation for her performance, but realized it was not really a performance. I am learning that many of the lost causes we try to help along the way are as much or more Monica's doing as mine.

Finally, Billy Spears said toward me, "Okay. I believe the lady. So why don't you tell me your story."

I gave Billy Spears the brief version of everything that had happened from the time Becky had walked into my office until we arrived at the Cockpit Lounge.

He asked, "So what do you want me to do?"

I replied, "There's something weird going on with Lone Star Aviation, and it's happening right around here in Harlingen. I believe that somehow you are the key to figuring this thing out. Why don't you tell us everything that led up to you losing your job."

Billy Spears explained that he had been an air traffic controller for over ten years. He told us that he was good at his job and took a lot of pride in it. He explained that—about three months previous—the Lone Star King Jet had flown down from Amarillo just as it does every forty-eight hours.

Billy said, "They claim it's some kind of training for new pilots, but it never made sense to me. It was my job to just keep them from running into each other up there. The Lone Star jet would fly down here, circle, do some patterns, some touch-and-goes on our runway, then land for fuel, and leave immediately for Amarillo. We always monitored them, but it's like one of those things you're used to seeing regularly. You don't pay close attention unless something unusual happens.

"On the day I got fired, I had cleared them for their maneuvers and their touch-and-goes. They flew off about 20 miles and did their normal, low-altitude patterns over the plains out there. That generally took them out of my radar range because they were so low. I was used to this, because it happened the same way every other day I worked. They radioed and asked for clearance to land and take on fuel, and I gave them permission just like I always did. I expected them to pop onto the radar 20 miles west where they had been flying their low-level patterns. All of a sudden, they were on my screen 30 miles to the south and crossing in front of a big American Airlines plane coming in from Mexico City."

Billy Spears blew out a deep breath and continued his story as if he were reliving it. "I went into the standard drill for near-misses. Both pilots were good, but it was really close. I got them on the ground, and the Lone Star plane refueled and was gone before the FAA boys could even get a report. The American Airlines guy was a jerk and wanted my job. They found a half bottle of bourbon I had in my desk drawer that I only drank from after my shift, but that was enough to make all fingers point my way."

I asked, "So, what really happened?"

Billy sighed and said, "I wish I could tell you. The official report says I blacked out or wasn't paying attention while the Lone Star jet flew 20 miles east and thirty miles south. But

I can tell you, that didn't happen. I was on top of it every second."

Monica asked, "What possible explanation could there be?"

Spears replied, "Folks, that's why I'm sitting here today trying to forget the whole thing. I appreciate your interest, but unless you can tell me how Lone Star's King Jet can be two places at the same time, there's no one that's gonna help me."

We bought Billy Spears a drink and talked a little longer, but when it was obvious we were at a dead end, Monica and I told him good-bye and walked out of the bar. Our cab driver was waiting for us and held the back door open as we got in.

He asked, "Back to the airport, sir?"

After a pause, I heard Monica say, "That will be fine." Monica knows that there are times when I am trying to visualize something in my head or solve a problem, and I am out of touch with the world around me. It's a skill akin to what John and I had learned about experiencing my environment. I simply become a part of everything around me, and instead of being on the outside looking in, I am living inside the puzzle that I am trying to solve.

Before I was really aware of what was going on around me, Monica and I were in our first-class seats 25,000 feet in the air, on our way back through Dallas.

I took a deep breath to relax and heard Monica say, "Welcome back, stranger. Have you got anything figured out yet?"

I replied, "Not yet, but I'm hoping there will be a clue on Franklin's video tape."

Our connection through Dallas/Ft. Worth airport was uneventful, which is always a rare and welcomed blessing. As the plane leveled off at its cruising altitude for its short flight to Amarillo, our flight attendant served Monica and me drinks.

Monica said, "Here's to the good times."

I replied, "And the best people."

We touched glasses and drank.

#. #. #.

At the dinner honoring John and me as returning war heroes of some type, I felt more like a zoo animal on display. Everyone shuffled by to meet John and to yell something casual toward me, careful not to touch on anything serious or meaningful so as to not put their foot in their mouth. I have never understood why people find it necessary to yell at a blind person, but it is one of the mysteries of life I no longer find insulting, but instead ironic enough to be comical.

John and I got through the dinner, and as my mother had promised, we left early for the dessert gathering at home. As we walked out to the church parking lot, I noticed John was never more than a few inches away from me and talked whenever we were walking. This was a pattern we had developed during the long weeks of rehab in California, but he seemed even more cautious with all of the strange people and unfamiliar surroundings.

He seemed to read my thoughts and commented, "Okie, I hope you don't mind, but I'm sticking close to your side 'cause this leg is really tired and could give out any minute."

John and I both knew that was a lie, but those are the lies we tell ourselves and friends like John in order to keep the world spinning in its orbit.

The intimate gathering at home became more and more uncomfortable as people departed for the evening, and it became obvious to everyone left that the point of the gathering was to get Mary Ann and me in the same place at the same time. Finally, Mary Ann took my hand and said, "Do you want to go for a walk, Jake?"

Feeling the old familiar patterns rush back between us, I forgot everything that had happened a world away and a lifetime ago. We held hands and walked down the front steps and along the familiar driveway of my parents' home. As we began walking along the sidewalk, Mary Ann said, "Jake, it's good to have you home. I prayed every day that you would be home safe and sound."

I released some of the anger boiling up in me and said, "Well, God didn't see fit to answer your prayers, did he?"

Mary Ann became agitated and said, "Jake, I didn't mean— well, you know—it's just that I don't know what to say."

We walked along in silence, and finally, I said, "Mary Ann, I'm sorry. This isn't your fault, and it's not your problem."

She replied cautiously, "I'd like to help if I could."

As I was mentally planning a way to explain to Mary Ann that I would not and could not hold her to any long-ago, teenage promise that we would get married and live happily-ever-after, I felt a terrible twisting and grinding in my right ankle followed by a tremendous blow to the top of my head and my face. Everything went silent.

#. #. #.

As the flight attendant touched my shoulder and asked me to fasten my seat belt for landing, I realized that I had been sleeping. Our plane landed in Amarillo on time, and Franklin was there like clockwork to meet us. He drove us back to our motel, and we agreed to order room service and then watch the video that had been shot of Lone Star's King Jet hangar over the past 24 hours.

We sat in our normal spots in my room and ate the room service dinner. Franklin and I had ordered club sandwiches, and Monica had a chicken Caesar salad. We all had Corona beer with lime. We fudged slightly on the not-talking-business-at-dinner rule as Monica and I filled Franklin in on the details of our day in Harlingen.

Franklin told us that he had been able to retrieve our video tape, start a new one which would monitor the hangar throughout the night and until noon the next day, and replace the air filter. It had all been uneventful, and Franklin felt he could get in and out several more times using his air conditioning and heating service front.

The video camera we use for such occasions is specialized in that it can record at any speed, including one slow enough to just bring up a few frames a second. It makes the image jerky, but allows us to monitor a scene for up to 24 hours.

Franklin cleared away the dinner dishes, and set the room service tray outside my door. We each settled back in anticipation of what secrets the video tape might unlock.

CHAPTER 20

Franklin turned on the TV and started the VCR he had rented from the motel office. As there was no sound on the video, I knew that Monica would fill me in on the details in much the same way that blind people enjoy movies on the Narrative Television Network.

Monica said, "We have a great view of the entire end of the hangar and the surrounding area. All the doors are closed, and there is no one around."

Since the slow-speed recorder only taped two images per second, Franklin was able to fast forward rapidly until there was some activity at the King Jet hangar. After a few moments of fast forwarding, Monica said, "Okay, there is one of those dark vans approaching. It says Lone Star Aviation on the side.

I'm unable to see the driver or anyone else inside. Two men are getting out, and they rush inside the hangar through the smaller door to the right of the huge doors where the plane goes in and out. The two men are wearing mirrored sunglasses and what looks like pilot or crew caps. The only description I can offer is that they are very dark-skinned, maybe Mexicans or South Americans."

The image resumed its inactivity, simply showing the long shot of the hangar with the black van parked outside. Franklin fast forwarded until Monica said, "Okay, there. We have the large doors opening, and the King Jet is visible in the shadows inside the hangar. Now the jet is moving through the large doors onto the tarmac. The large doors are closing, and the jet is taxiing to the runway."

I asked Franklin to pause the video, and I had Monica write down the registration number from the tail section of the jet as well as the tag number from the van parked outside. Once Monica told us she had the numbers, Franklin continued playing the video.

Monica said, "The jet has taxied out of the picture and onto the runway. Everything on the image is now still again, the doors are closed, and the van is parked outside."

Franklin fast forwarded the video until Monica said, "Okay, stop here. The large hangar doors are beginning to open."

Franklin let us know that—according to the counter on the VCR—he had fast forwarded through over four hours of real time video since the jet had left the picture.

Monica continued, "The jet is returning and taxiing into the hangar where it was before. It is shadowy inside, but it seems they are beginning to unload the plane. Two dark-skinned men in coveralls are coming out of the large doors and moving toward the back of the van. They are opening the back doors of the van and getting inside. Now a group of dark-skinned men in coveralls are coming out of the large hangar doors, each carrying a box about the size of a standard microwave oven. They each get into the back of the van and are out of sight. The men go back and forth shuttling the boxes from the jet to the van.

"Now the hangar doors begin to close as the last group of dark-skinned men in coveralls gets into the back of the van and close the back doors. The small door opens and the two dark-skinned men who arrived in the van earlier wearing the mirrored sunglasses and flight caps get into the front seat of the van, and the van drives away. The screen is now back to a long shot of the hangar, the doors are closed, and no one is stirring."

Franklin fast forwarded the tape and continued until he said, "Sir, the picture is getting darker as the sun is dropping. The lights come on around the perimeter of the hangar illuminating the entire area. As I fast forward through the night, the only activity around the King Jet hangar is a couple of passes by Lone Star security vehicles and airport guards. The hangar remains closed with no activity through the early morning and until the tape ends during the middle of the day. Do we want to go through it again, sir?"

I thought for a few moments trying to get the visual images in my mind so that I could replay them on my own without the tape and VCR. I responded, "No, Franklin, I think that will be enough."

Monica asked, "So, what's going on, Jake? Did they pick up the Mexicans and the boxes in Harlingen or were they already in the hangar?"

"I don't know," I replied, "but we're going to find out. Franklin, we have a tape which should monitor the next King Jet training run the day after tomorrow?"

"Correct, sir," Franklin replied.

It was getting late, and we'd each had a long day. I suggested we retire for the evening and meet for breakfast in the morning.

Franklin asked, "Would that be bagels in the room or Aunt Molly's Kitchen or something new, sir?"

"I think the bagels, Franklin," I responded.

Franklin and Monica each took their leave through their individual connecting doors into their rooms. I lay back on my bed and let the images as described by Monica play over and over in my mind. There was something there right in front of me, but I just couldn't bring it into mental focus. But it was there, nevertheless.

# # #

I became aware of my surroundings and registered the now-familiar hospital sounds. I had awakened groggily so many times on the hospital ship, I was used to the sounds of my surroundings coming to me a little at a time. When enough of the sounds had come together to give me a clearer image, I realized something was different. I was not on the hospital ship, but the sounds and smells were certainly that of a hospital.

My head felt about three sizes too large, and I reached my hand toward my head to find out what the situation might be. Then I heard a familiar voice that let me know I was going to be all right no matter where I was.

"Good morning, Okie. We had a bit of a rough night here in the hospital, but these nurses here in Tulsa are a whole lot better than the ones on the hospital ship."

Instantly, I remembered my parents' home, the church dinner, and walking with Mary Ann through the neighborhood. That was the last thing I could remember.

I asked, "What happened, John?"

He replied, "Well, it seems that while you and Mary Ann were walking along, you stepped off the edge of the sidewalk where there was a bit of a drop-off. You managed to sprain your ankle pretty bad and fall forward into a brick fence. You have a mild concussion and took a few stitches along your hairline. Your nose is broken, and your face is swollen rather badly. I personally think it's a pretty good look for you, and you'll be happy to know that the brick fence sustained no damage."

I lay there and let the realization of what had happened fill in the blank spots in my memory.

"How is Mary Ann?" I asked.

"Well, she blames herself for the whole thing. She was down the hall in the waiting room crying most of the night. I tried to explain to her that it wasn't her fault, and after everything you've been through, this is just like a walk in the park. But, I don't think she's buying any of it."

John and I remained in silence for a long time. A long silence is only comfortable among the best of friends. Casual relationships have to be propped up with small talk, but it was enough for John and me to simply know that we were there together.

"Do you want to talk to her?" John asked.

"What do you think I should do?" I questioned.

"Well, she's been asking for you all night, and I told her I would let her know when you woke up. It's going to be hard to keep her out of here. She feels really guilty about letting you fall like that. I told her that you were very capable of falling on your own without her help, but I think the two of you need to talk about a lot more than last night."

I thought about Mary Ann and what she must be going through. I realized that at one point in another lifetime, I probably had loved her, at least to the extent that I had the capacity to know and understand love at that time. As I lay there, I knew that I didn't love her now, but that was more a result of the fact that I didn't love anyone or anything, including myself. I felt that my life had been ruined, and I was damaging everyone around me. The only honorable thing I could do was release her now so that she would suffer as little as possible.

I said, "I guess you better bring her in, John."

#. #. #.

The phone woke me, and I realized that, once again, I had been reliving a memory of a quarter century ago in my dreams. I picked up the phone and heard Monica say, "Good morning, boss. We're heading out for bagels and coffee. Do you need anything else?"

"No," I responded.

She said, "We'll be back in about 15 or 20 minutes."

I got up, showered, dressed, and got ready for the day.

After we had consumed our morning meal, and the silence had fallen over us, I knew it was my turn to come up with the plan of action.

I said, "Before we do anything further, I've got to call Harlingen to try to get a line on those boxes and the guys in the coveralls."

I moved to the phone, dialed directory assistance, and

then dialed the main number at the Harlingen Airport. With Monica and Franklin listening on, I went into my act.

"Good morning, ma'am. I am calling from Lone Star Aviation, and I need to talk to whoever refueled our King Jet there yesterday."

She transferred me to the fuel station, and a tired-sounding young man answered, "This is Steve."

I responded, "Steve, I'm calling from Lone Star headquarters up here in Amarillo. I need to get some information on the shipment and passengers that were picked up in Harlingen there yesterday. I know it's not your problem, but our pilot's out of pocket right now, and I've got to get this paperwork turned in before noon today. So I was hoping you might help me."

He responded, "I don't know what you're talking about. I refueled the King Jet myself just like I always do. The plane landed, they taxied to my fuel station, they took on a full load of fuel, they opened the door long enough to have the pilot sign my paperwork, and they took off for Amarillo. I can guarantee you they didn't get any cargo or passengers here."

I managed to get confusion and frustration into my voice and said, "You know, it's really hard to get good people these days. I'm just going to send the paperwork in incomplete, and let the chips fall where they may."

I thanked Steve for his time, and we hung up.

I told Monica and Franklin what I had learned from Steve, and we sat in confused silence for a while. Monica voiced all of our thoughts when she said, "Jake, what is going on?"

heard Mary Ann's voice as she entered the room. "Hello, Jake. How are you feeling?"

I made an effort to sound better than I felt. "Oh, I'm feeling fine."

John said, "I think I'll stretch this old leg of mine, and then I'll wait right outside in case either of you need me."

Mary Ann stood alongside my bed and took my hand. She said, "Jake, I am so very, very sorry. It was all my fault. I was just so focused on what we were talking about, I didn't watch where you were stepping. The next thing I knew, your foot had slipped off the edge of the sidewalk, and you had fallen into a brick wall. You were unconscious, so they had to call an ambulance for you. Your parents and John sat with you here all night. I felt so guilty I couldn't face them, so I just waited down the hall."

I said, "Mary Ann, it's no big deal. After everything I've been through, it really doesn't matter. But there is something I need to talk to you about. You know, we've always been really close, and if someone had asked me before I left for Vietnam, I would have told them I loved you and wanted to spend the rest of my life with you."

"You know I've always felt the same way about you, Jake," Mary Ann interjected.

I took a deep breath and then continued. "I know. You've always been great, but that was then, and this is now. The Jacob Dyer you knew died somewhere over the jungle in Vietnam when our helicopter was hit. I don't know who I am now, but it's not the same guy that you knew then. I don't know what I'm going to do with my life or even what I can do."

Mary Ann released the frustration that had obviously built up and said, "Jacob Dyer, you act like you're the only one affected by this. I know that this whole thing has been torture for you, but it hasn't been easy for all of us who care about you to be stuck here in Tulsa just hearing occasional updates on your condition. Your parents and I were really hurt when you didn't want us to come and visit you at the rehab hospital in California. I don't buy John's story about some hospital policy not allowing us to come."

A silence stretched out between us, and finally I said, "I'm sorry. I know this has been hard on everybody, and if it ever gets any better, it's not going to be for a long time yet. I guess what I'm trying to say is that the Jacob Dyer you may have felt a commitment to is no longer here, and . . ."

Mary Ann interrupted, "Do you think I'm the same person that kissed you good-bye at the airport fourteen months ago? Trying to act like everything was normal while being obsessed with the thoughts of what was going on with you? And then when I heard you had been hit and that you were blind, all my visions of living happily ever after faded away, and the Mary Ann you left at the Tulsa Airport faded away, too. So, even if I don't know what you're trying to say here, at least I feel I understand where you're coming from."

Our silence resumed, and I wasn't sure what to say. But I knew that something needed to be said, and the time for saying it had arrived. "Mary Ann, I think I understand that both of us are different people than we were back in high school. That would probably be true even if I'd come home normal. But this thing is like an octopus. It has so many legs that go so many directions, I don't even yet understand what living the rest of my life in the dark is going to mean to me or the people around me."

Mary Ann said in a voice that made me proud of the person she had become, "Jake, I don't know what you're trying to say, but let's leave it like this. I believe we loved each other before. I don't know what would have happened if things kept going the way they were, but they didn't. So let's both relax and get to know each other again and find out if the Jacob you've become can get along with the Mary Ann I've become."

I felt a sense of relief as I laid there and held her hand. I also realized that I felt closer to her than I ever had before. Sometimes being released from a commitment unchains the emotions that you wanted to feel when the commitment was made.

#. #. #.

Monica interrupted my daydreaming as I heard her ask, "Jake, where do we go from here?"

I thought for a few moments and said, "I think I might be beginning to understand what's going on here, but we have got to have rock-solid proof before we're going to get any help in this thing."

I let things play out in my mind for a few moments until they formed themselves into a short-term plan. I asked, "Franklin, have you ever had any rifle training?"

A brief rumble was followed by his response. "Yes, sir. I can shoot quite well. I spent a lot of time shooting targets and hunting with Mr. Henson. Is there someone who needs shooting, sir?"

I replied, "Not yet, but I'd like you to go out today and buy a high-powered pellet gun."

Franklin sniffed and questioned, "Did you say a pellet gun, sir?"

"Yes, a pellet gun—you know a kid's air rifle—one that you can shoot fairly accurately from 150 to 200 feet away."

Franklin asked, "How accurately, sir?"

I thought for a minute and responded, "Oh, if you could hit a dinner plate at 200 feet, I think we'll be fine."

Franklin asked, "When will I need to be proficient with this pellet gun, sir?"

I answered, "Tomorrow morning when Lone Star's King Jet comes out of the hangar for its routine flight."

Monica asked, "Will I need a pellet gun, too, Jake? If we're going to shoot down a jet with a pellet gun, we might need two."

I answered, "No, you and I are going to play reporter and photographer and get an interview with Max and Jim Ed Leland. Did you bring your camera?"

Monica answered, "Sure. With the bag full of attachments,

I can make a convincing photographer."

I asked Monica to call the Lelands' office building downtown and tell them we were with *Texas People* magazine. She was to tell them we were just in town for the day and wanted to get some photos and do an interview for a feature. Monica went into her room through the connecting door and closed it behind her.

Franklin said, "If there's nothing else here, sir, I'll go and make the arrangements we discussed."

We agreed that Franklin would take our vehicle, and Monica and I would catch a cab to and from the Lelands' office building downtown. The cab would be consistent with our story of being reporters from out of town. Franklin and I agreed that we would all meet back at the motel to compare notes and have dinner together later.

Franklin left, and as I was sitting down to review the plans in my mind, Monica opened the connecting door and said, "They will meet us at one o'clock this afternoon for an interview and photos. I talked to Max Leland, himself, and he sounded like he would walk on hot coals for some good publicity."

Monica and I rehearsed our roles as a magazine reporter and photographer, ordered a light room service lunch, and caught a cab to the Lelands' office tower downtown. As the cab let us out in front of the office tower, Monica took my arm and described the Leland Building. She said, "It is a large, mirrored glass tower with probably 30 floors. It appears to be one of the taller buildings around here."

We crossed the lobby which Monica described as office drab and caught the elevator to the top floor where Max and Jim Ed Leland conducted whatever business—legitimate or not—in which they were involved. We entered the waiting room, and a nice young lady told us she would let Max and Jim Ed know we had arrived.

While we were alone in the waiting room, Monica described photos of Max and Jim Ed displayed on the wall. She said, "Max appears to be about 55, short, and probably 20 pounds overweight. He has dark hair, probably a dye job. Jim Ed is taller and thin with a hatchet-like face. He does one of those disgusting comb-over jobs to hide his baldness. It does more to point out his baldness than anything else. Judging from the furnishings and artwork here in the office, these guys are doing well at something."

The receptionist returned and led us to a conference room where she got us seated. As she was walking out the door, she said, "Max and Jim Ed will be with you shortly."

Monica described the surroundings as board room ostentatious. She said, "There's enough leather in here to outfit an entire motorcycle gang."

We sat in silence and reviewed our individual roles in the upcoming drama. As I sat there, I wondered how many times over the years I had pretended to be someone else, either in person or on the phone. I realized that sometimes it is more comfortable to pretend to be someone else because during the role-play, you are entirely who you are pretending to be. When we are being ourselves, there are so many emotions in play that I feel some of the best acting ever done happens when we human beings are ourselves.

#. #. #.

Mary Ann stayed with me most of every day and night for the four days I was in the hospital. When I left, I had a limp and a headache the doctors assured me would both go away. I had a scar on my forehead which they assured me would not go away.

Over the next few weeks, Mary Ann and I got to know each other for who we had become instead of who we thought we were before. We realized that we had a friendship and a respect that had been unknown to us in our previous relationship; however, if there had been a spark of passion between us before, neither of us were able to find it again. I have suspected over the ensuing years that the passion had never been there before. It was something that we both wanted to be there because the books and movies told us it was supposed to be there.

Mary Ann and I became friends and remain so today. We leaned on one another heavily then, and less as time passed. But even now, I know that if I were to need a true friend on a moment's notice, Mary Ann would be there. We never really parted as lovers, we evolved into friends and stayed that way.

#. #. #.

My thoughts of Mary Ann were interrupted by the booming voices of Max and Jim Ed Leland entering the conference room. I shook hands with both of them and introduced them to Monica. I explained to them that I was blind and was a reporter for *Texas People* magazine. I don't usually tell people I can't see, because Monica and I have developed our roles so well over the years that it's not apparent to anyone that I can't see. In this situation, since I wasn't sure where we were going, I thought it would be wise to tell them of my blindness up front.

Monica explained she would be shooting some candid shots while the interview was going on. She sat both of the Lelands

159

in leather chairs across the table from me, got them situated, and began taking a few photos.

I sat back and prepared to question the two men who had ruined John's life, stolen his business, and probably killed him. I was more convinced than ever that they were guilty of my worst suspicions, but I had to figure out some way to trap them so that I could prove it.

I sensed the fear that a small animal must feel when he is used as bait for a dangerous predator.

CHAPTER 22

I tried to control the fear I felt as well as the anger that the Lelands brought out in me. It was difficult to forget everything that the brothers had done to John and Becky while I simply acted like a magazine reporter.

I took out a small pocket tape recorder I use for my reporter routine and started by asking, "You two have become quite famous, and you've come a long way from humble beginnings. What do you consider your most significant success to date?"

Max Leland answered, "Jim Ed and I feel that our greatest successes are the many civic projects we are able to undertake for our community."

Jim Ed chimed in, "We're just happy to do good work that makes a difference for our friends and neighbors."

I said, "Give us a feel for the type of businesses you own and operate."

Max said, "Well, of course, oil and gas—being here in West Texas. And then, there's the real estate developments, including resort property. And recently we've purchased a couple of small banks."

I cautiously said, "And I understand that you run an airline as well."

There was an awkward pause, and then Jim Ed said dismissively, "No, not really. We took over a small charter service a few years ago, but it hasn't done well, and it's barely operating today."

I asked, "Would that be Lone Star Aviation?"

Max shot back, "Yes, but like Jim Ed said, it's really not a part of this story."

I followed up with, "I had always heard that Lone Star Aviation was a powerful company and had done well over the years."

"Not really. It used to be a good company, but the son-in-law of the founder had run it into the ground before we bought it. It's really been a loser for us," Jim Ed responded.

There are times when you know you're on thin ice, and you just have to step out on it and hope for the best. At times like that, waiting around doesn't help the situation. You've got to simply forge ahead.

I asked, "If Lone Star is barely operating, why did the company, under your direction, go out and purchase one of the most expensive, private jets in the world? It's called a King Jet, I believe."

There was a long pause, and both brothers finally started to respond at the same time. Max overrode his brother and said,

"Well, Lone Star had a good reputation here in Texas, and we were hoping to save the company by purchasing a new jet for charter work. Unfortunately, it hasn't worked out, so we only use the King Jet for pilot training."

I pressed on. "Would those be the flights every-other-day to Harlingen and back? They seem rather mysterious to me, and I understand an air traffic controller got fired after losing track of your jet and narrowly avoiding a mid-air collision."

I heard Max Leland slam his fist on the table and say in a forceful tone, "I don't know what's going on, but your little lady friend here said we were doing a public relations piece on me and Jim Ed. But all you seem to want to talk about is Lone Star Aviation. I don't know what you think you're trying to find out, but it's not a part of this story."

I replied before I thought, "Well, sir, what I'm trying to find out is what happened to John Ivers and what he knew about what you two are doing with Lone Star Aviation."

Jim Ed responded in a low, menacing tone, "Listen to me, blind man. This interview is over. You and your lady friend can go out the same door you came in."

Monica was standing by my side. I stood up. She took my arm, and we headed for the door to the conference room. As we were walking back into the hall, I heard Max call out, "I've got a friend at *Texas People* magazine, and I'll have your jobs. I suggest you watch your step, harassing hard-working business people like us."

Monica and I got to the sidewalk in front of the Leland Building as quickly as possible. We finally found a cab—which are not plentiful in Amarillo—and directed the driver back to our motel.

Monica said, "Well, boss, I believe the gauntlet has been

thrown down. You definitely got their attention."

I replied, "Well, it wasn't exactly what I had intended, but I'm hoping they will make a mistake now."

As I reviewed the meeting with Max and Jim Ed Leland in my mind, Monica said cautiously, "Jake, there is a black sedan that seems to want to turn every time we do since we left the Leland Building."

We directed our driver to take a few minor detours, and Monica told me that the black sedan stayed right with us. Finally, I said to the driver, "Just take us back to the Armadillo Lodge. They are going to know who we are soon enough."

The cab driver let us out in the parking lot, and we paid him. As we were walking up the stairs, Monica said, "Our favorite black sedan is parked right across the parking lot. There seem to be two Neanderthal types very interested in us."

Monica and I went into my room and tried to relax. As we were sorting out everything that had happened to us, Franklin returned from his shopping and target practice mission.

Monica said, "Welcome back, handsome. Did you notice a black sedan across the parking lot?"

Franklin emitted a brief sniff and responded, "Yes, Miss, it was parked facing our rooms, and there seem to be two disreputable-looking gentlemen observing our movements."

I felt good about the fact that we were rattling someone's cage, even though we weren't sure exactly what we were doing. Franklin assured me that he felt confidence in his ability to hit a target at 60 yards.

I suggested that we each get a little rest and then change for dinner. Monica suggested a seafood restaurant called the Gulf Coast which she had seen earlier. We agreed that we would leave at six and dine at the Gulf Coast.

Franklin and Monica went to their rooms through their connecting doors, and I was left alone with my thoughts. For about the millionth time in the last 25 years, I asked myself how I had gotten into this line of work and why a blind person should be spending his life trying to find things that other people can't.

# # #

John and I spent several months together, and during that time I got acquainted—in a new way—with my parents' home, their neighborhood, and the city of Tulsa. I felt reasonably comfortable getting around town utilizing buses, cabs, and my white cane.

During one of our many long walks, John asked, "Well, Okie, what do you think you're going to do for a living? You've been loafing around here long enough."

I was shocked. I had no idea how to respond to him, because working had never occurred to me. When you're not sure whether or not you want to continue living, pursuing a career is not a high priority.

I finally responded, "John, I'm not sure anybody would hire me, and I can't imagine what I would do working for anybody else, anyway."

John sounded pleased as he announced, "That's exactly what I was thinking, so I kinda figured we would go into business together."

I asked, "What in the world are you talking about, John?"

He responded in the tone I always loved, "Now, Okie, I think you're getting skeptical on me again. You know how you get sometimes. I just want you to relax and realize that I have had an inspired idea, and if you'll just have a little faith in yourself and my inspired idea, you might be amazed."

\#. \#. \#.

After an enjoyable dinner at the Gulf Coast, during which we observed our rule about not discussing work, we came back to my room at the Armadillo Lodge to make plans for the next day. The black sedan was with us the entire evening, but they didn't seem to want anything other than to follow us.

We ordered some coffee from room service. Franklin and I took our normal chairs, and Monica perched on the edge of my bed. I began by saying, "There's a big difference between what we think and what we know. All we know for sure is there's something very strange going on at Lone Star Aviation and, particularly, with the King Jet. We think that there are drugs involved and illegal aliens, but we can't prove it, and we can't even explain how they're doing it. We've got to catch Max and Jim Ed Leland doing something illegal that we can prove beyond the shadow of a doubt."

Monica asked, "How do we do that, Jake?"

While I was finalizing our next steps in my mind, Franklin answered a knock at the door and brought in a tray containing our coffee. He poured three cups and added cream and sugar to everyone's taste.

I sipped my coffee and said, "Franklin, tomorrow morning I need you to get back into the attic above the office; but you've got to be careful, because our little magazine interview today has alerted the Lelands. I will take Monica to breakfast in a cab in order to draw off our two friends in the parking lot. When you get into the attic, leave the video tape rolling. When the King Jet comes out of its hangar, I want you to take the pellet gun and shoot a part of the tail section that has been painted."

Franklin performed a rarity which was a low rumble with a sniff and said, "Sir, am I to understand that you want me to shoot a jet with my newly-acquired pellet gun?"

I responded, "That is correct, Franklin."

He replied, "But, sir, the most I could hope to do to the jet would be maybe chip the paint slightly or make a small dent in the surface of the metal. I can't imagine that . . ."

I interrupted Franklin saying, "That's exactly what I'm hoping you can accomplish, Franklin. Once you have finished, I want you to get all of our camera equipment and your pellet gun and get out of there carefully, removing any sign that you were ever there."

Franklin said, "Very good, sir. I have an air conditioner compressor box that I can fit everything into as I'm leaving. I don't foresee any difficulties."

I said, "While you're doing that, Monica and I will be working on a little party of our own. People who have done as much as the Lelands deserve to get proper recognition."

## CHAPTER 23

The next morning, Monica and I enjoyed a wonderful breakfast at Aunt Molly's Kitchen, and we had the satisfaction of knowing that our two friends in the black sedan were parked in the hot sun observing the front of the restaurant. Knowing that the temperature was already well into the 90s, Monica suggested, "Well, since we're here, don't you think we should have one more cup of coffee, Jake?"

We took our time and returned to our motel late in the morning. Monica and I were working on a preliminary contact list of government officials and media representatives when Franklin returned. He quickly set up the VCR and played the new surveillance tape he had retrieved from the attic.

I asked, "Did you have any trouble getting in and out?"

Franklin replied, "There were a few more people about, sir, but when I told the gentleman in the office that the compressor would probably not last through the day, and since it was going to be over a hundred, I was certain they would want me to replace it. I am pleased to report no major difficulties."

Franklin fast forwarded through the video of the King Jet hangar over the past 24 hours. There was nothing remarkable until the King Jet emerged from the hangar just as before, and at the appropriate moment, Franklin was able to freeze-frame the image, and Monica discovered a small scratch and dent in the paint along the tail section of the jet.

Monica sounded excited as she said, "In one frame, everything's okay, and in the next, the scratch and dent are just there."

I responded, "Great job, Franklin."

A low rumble was his only response.

I thought for a minute and said, "Monica, I need for you to get all your photo equipment including the long-range lens together. Franklin, I need you to take Monica out to the airport and find some inconspicuous place where she can take a photograph of the scratched and dented tail section when the plane returns from Harlingen."

Monica asked, "Boss, why do we want a photograph of the pellet gun damage when we already have the video?"

I replied, "If my suspicion is correct, that will be clear to you. If I'm not correct, we are all in deep sewage. But you'll have to hurry, because the jet will be returning shortly."

Within a few moments, Monica had emerged with all of her camera equipment, and as she and Franklin were preparing to leave, Franklin asked, "And what about our friends in the sedan, sir?"

I thought for a minute and laughed, "Franklin, you won't be driving the Rolls Royce. We have a four-wheel-drive vehicle. I'm certain you can find somewhere to go that our friends in the sedan won't be able to follow."

Franklin let out a large rumble and said, "Very good, sir."

Franklin and Monica left, and I lit a vanilla-flavored cigar and sat back in one of the easy chairs to evaluate our situation.

#. #. #.

The business that is now known as Dyer Straits Lost and Found started with John and me recovering some stolen planes which had been reported as crashed to the insurance company. We discovered that the planes had not been crashed, but the thieves had simply hauled wreckage to a site where they reported the airplane down.

John did some fancy flying, and I worked the telephones and allowed a few people to get under the wrong impression, and before I knew it, we had solved the mystery. The insurance company was so grateful that they gave us a fee sufficient to support us both and our start-up business for several years. We had a few more successes, and I was just feeling a little bit of comfort with our working relationship the day that John dropped the bomb.

He said, "Okie, we've been doing pretty good here, but you don't need me any more. It's time for you to go it alone. Becky and I are getting married, and I'm going to start flying for her dad's company down in Texas."

I was in shock. I felt that John had been carrying us both, and I couldn't imagine he was going to leave me alone after all that time.

I screamed at him, "If you were going to leave me now, why didn't you just let me die in the jungle?"

#. #. #.

My painful memory was interrupted when Franklin and Monica returned. Monica was whistling, which is generally reserved for when she has located what she calls a killer dress with matching shoes on sale, or she has performed a difficult task exceedingly well.

I asked, "Well, how did it go?"

Monica said, "No sweat, boss. Got the film right here."

"Any trouble?" I asked.

Franklin sniffed and responded, "Our four-wheel-drive vehicle was able to drive down an embankment and across a stream. I fear that the sedan was simply not up to the task, sir."

Monica chimed in with, "Frankie dropped me off near the Lone Star hangar to get my photos, then he drove around the perimeter of the airport and came back to pick me up. We felt I would be less noticeable without a vehicle. I got my photos, and as Franklin was approaching to pick me up, a Lone Star security guy tried to grab my camera."

I couldn't help the concerned tone that crept into my voice. "What did you do then?"

A hearty rumble sounded as Franklin replied, "Sir, I fear that before I could get out of the sports utility vehicle and come to Miss Monica's aid, the security guard in question sustained a serious groin injury by way of Miss Monica's cowboy boot. We drove back here without further incident."

I asked Monica, "What's the easiest and fastest way to get those pictures developed?"

She replied, "There's a one-hour place downtown. Why don't we drop off the film, grab a bite of lunch, and pick up the pictures on the way back?

As Franklin drove us out of the parking lot, he commented with a brief sniff, "Sir, it's nice to take a leisurely drive without a black sedan hounding one in the background at all times."

After a pleasant lunch at a local Italian spot, Franklin drove us back to the one-hour photo shop. Monica ran inside to retrieve her pictures, and she was silent as she climbed into the back seat with me. I decided to wait for her response.

She sounded forlorn as she said, "Boss, I don't know what to say. I had my best lens, and I took pictures of the entire tail section, but the scratch and dent from the pellet gun is simply not there."

Franklin shuffled through the photos and said, "Sir, I can assure you Miss Monica's pictures capture the entire tail section, particularly the area where the scratch and dent were; but the plane is in perfect condition. I don't know what happened to the scratch and dent."

I replied joyously, "I'm sure the scratch and dent are in great shape and will go down in the record as the most significant factor in restoring Lone Star Aviation to Becky Ivers."

I had Franklin stop by the Amarillo Chamber of Commerce while we were downtown. I asked Monica to go in and see about getting us a complete directory of all Amarillo media, government offices, and law enforcement agencies. As Franklin drove us back to our motel, I mentally put the final touches on my plans for the event we would be hosting for the Lelands.

CHAPTER 24

uring the rest of the afternoon, Monica and Franklin were dedicated to converting our three adjoining motel rooms into our command post for the counter assault designed to liberate Lone Star Aviation from Max and Jim Ed Leland. Monica located and made arrangements to rent a computer, printer, and fax machine. Franklin installed all of the equipment, and Monica double-checked to make sure everything was in readiness.

I sat back in one of the chairs in my room and tried to stay out of their way. I lit a Jamaican cigar and mentally went step by step through the operation that would be set up the next day and climax the following morning.

This operation was like a set of dominoes poised to fall in

line. If everything came off perfectly, it would work; however, if any single step was the slightest bit off, the whole plan would be blown. I didn't want to think about the consequences of failure for Monica, Franklin, and me, much less Becky Ivers.

I believed that I had learned what John Ivers had discovered just before he was killed. The only advantage I had was that I knew what the Lelands had done to John. Sometimes knowing the consequences of failure forces one's actions to be precise the first time. It's the difference between walking the length of a wooden plank six inches off the ground or sixty feet in the air. It's the same plank, but the consequences of failure are the difference between life and death.

#. #. #.

The tension hung in the air between John and me. It was a living thing. I had let all of my torture and frustration burst out in one brief statement. For the first time since our helicopter was hit in Vietnam, I wished for something more than to recover my sight. I wished I could take back the venomous words I had screamed at John.

Finally, unable to bear the silence any longer, I said, "John, look, I'm sorry."

I could feel the tears running down my face as I continued. "I don't know what to do, I don't know where to go, and you've been my life-line through everything. The thought of having you leave me here to run this business and live my life alone is more than I can take."

John laughed and said, "Okie, we had a deal. That was, we would get through this thing together. We would live together or die together. So, what makes you think I'm going to leave you stranded now? I have done my best to be there for you every step of the way just like I know you will be there for me if I ever need you. But now, old buddy, the best thing I can do to be there for you is to let you figure out you can do this on your own."

I said shakily, "John, I feel like I'm walking a tight-rope, and you are taking away my safety net."

John said thoughtfully, "Maybe there's a way we can have our cake and eat it, too. What if you and I could make a deal that would allow you to go it alone but still have the safety net?"

#. #. #.

Sometimes, before you go into battle or are faced with an intense crisis, the best thing to do is to make sure you are in complete readiness and then get totally away from the situation and clear your mind. Somehow, I believe Monica knows this although, to my knowledge, she has never been in battle—at least the kind that changed me from the innocent, young boy I was into the Jacob Dyer I have become.

Monica breezed back into my room through her connecting door and perched on the corner of my bed. She said triumphantly, "Well, boss, all systems are ready to launch and good to go."

As Franklin stood by, she recounted her entire list of preparations and then explained how the system had been double-checked. Then she came out of left field saying, "Now that that's all done, we've been cooped up in this place for too long. Jake, my social life is a disaster since we got to Amarillo. I've got a reputation to uphold, so I've planned an appropriate outing for us."

Franklin emitted a curious but satisfied rumble, and I asked, "Well, Princess Monica, would you please fill us in on the details of this proposed outing?"

Monica explained that this was not a proposed outing, but had actually already been set in motion. She said, "You told me to check out the computer system, so I got on the Internet and searched all of the restaurants in this area. I found one bed-and-breakfast west of town that is owned by a retired chef from New York. I tested our fax machine by sending him an order for the preparation of a deluxe picnic basket to be prepared, including suitable champagne and all the appropriate trimmings. I asked him to fax a confirmation back to me so that I would know that our machine was printing on this end. Therefore, friends and colleagues, I have—in one fell swoop—completed our preparations for our upcoming mission, tested our equipment, and finalized arrangements for the ultimate outing."

Monica went on to explain that via the Internet, she had also found information about a beautiful little lake forty miles west of town, so we could pick up our picnic extravaganza at 7:45 and be picnicking lakeside in time to enjoy sunset over the lake.

Franklin said enthusiastically, "Quite impressive, Miss Monica."

I agreed, and we each went to dress appropriately for the evening.

Franklin, using the sixth sense of all great chauffeurs, found the remote bed-and-breakfast without detour. He opened the door for us, and Monica and I got out and stood in the driveway. As she took my arm, she described our surroundings.

"If I didn't know we were just a little ways outside Amarillo, Texas, I would think we were a million miles away. The house, itself, is designed like a Swiss chalet, and the gardens surrounding it have been created and tended by a real genius."

As we walked around to the side entrance, we met Chef Bernárd. He was immediately captivated by Monica, a circumstance I find understandable, and we were given a full tour of his world-class kitchen.

He had prepared—and packed into an antique wicker picnic hamper—caviar, cold chicken, freshly baked breads, several vegetable trays, fresh fruit, and some exotic pastries for dessert. He had topped it all off with imported Swiss chocolates and two bottles of chilled champagne. He had supplied china, silver, crystal champagne glasses, and even a large blanket for the occasion.

Monica thanked him and promised we would bring everything back late that evening. He assured her there was no hurry, and Monica bestowed him with a kiss on the cheek for good measure. At that point, I believe he would have given her the entire bed-and-breakfast if she had asked.

Franklin drove us out to the lake and located an ideal spot for the occasion. He and Monica arranged our feast as I stood off to the side and enjoyed the fresh air and a surprisingly cool breeze off the lake.

As we had our first champagne toast of the evening, Monica described the sun setting over the lake to me. In my previous life, sunsets had always been one of my favorite sights. They are not so much the end of one day as the promise of a new one. With the self-training John and I had done in experiencing our environment, I enjoy so many things I had missed before, and the privilege of having someone I care about describe a visual image to me is something I treasure. That evening, having Monica share her eyes with me to enjoy the sunset, created a rare and treasured memory.

My favorite regular dining experience is enjoyed weekly at

an award-winning restaurant known as the Duck Club in a first-class hotel in south Tulsa. I have my own corner table, and Hamid—the best waiter in the world—presents incomparable food and wine with world-class service. He is more than a great waiter; he is a great friend.

Our picnic wasn't quite the Duck Club, but all things considered, it was extremely close. We ate and drank to excess and talked of life, hope, and the dreams of things to come.

After we had drained the last of the champagne with a final toast to honoring old debts, Franklin packed up everything as Monica and I took a brief walk along the lakeshore. I enjoyed a special cigar given to me by an old friend the previous Christmas. It was almost like having him join us at the lakeshore.

Back at the bed-and-breakfast, Monica heaped her praises on Chef Bernárd, which he soaked up like a sponge. I shook his hand, and Franklin emitted the rare rumble of admiration.

On the ride back to Amarillo, Monica held my hand, and we listened to Chopin on the stereo. I felt my mind drifting back to the task we would face beginning tomorrow. Monica sensed the tension building in me and said, "Jake, the best advice you ever gave me was that once you have prepared everything and are ready to do your best, that is all you can do. Then you just relax, and let it happen. Boss, you are the best there is at whatever it is we do, and Becky Ivers is lucky to have a friend like you."

I thought about Becky, John, and the promises made long ago—made long ago, but not forgotten.

## CHAPTER 25

The next morning, we met in my room as arranged at eight thirty for bagels and coffee. I laid out the plan and the steps we would be taking to try to get from here to there, and said, "The whole key to this operation is going to be to have the right people showing up at the King Jet hangar at the right time—without discovering that we set it up—and keep everyone in place until the Lelands are exposed. We are going to have to stop the jet from leaving for Harlingen tomorrow morning and hold it at the hangar until the time it would normally return to Amarillo. This will mean keeping everyone in their places for approximately four hours."

I had Monica prepare a press release that would be faxed to all Amarillo area television, radio, and newspaper outlets.

The press release was to announce the fact that Lone Star Aviation was expanding its operation and acquiring a new King Jet. The jet would be arriving at the Amarillo Airport at approximately noon the following day. At that time, the new King Jet and Max and Jim Ed Leland would be available for a photo opportunity and interviews.

I told Monica to begin faxing immediately, starting with TV and radio, followed by the print media. Franklin had arranged—through some electronic wizardry I failed to understand—to have the fax machine transmit our press releases without anyone being able to tell where they came from.

While Monica and Franklin were alerting the media to what I knew would be a great story, I prepared to make the first of several critical phone calls. I dialed the number that Monica had given me for the West Texas office of the Environmental Protection Agency. The phone was answered efficiently on the second ring.

"EPA. Agent Timmons speaking."

I said, "Is this *the* Agent Timmons?"

After a brief pause, Timmons sounded confused when he said, "What do you mean *the* Timmons?"

I responded with, "Well, sir, here in Washington, we've heard exemplary reports about Agent Timmons down in Texas. The word is, *Timmons is really going places*, but I never expected to get to talk to you myself."

Timmons attempted to sound modest. "I'm just trying to do my job the best I know how."

I said, "Glad to hear it, Timmons, because we have a very delicate situation. Here in Washington, we have received some disturbing reports about Lone Star Aviation. I believe they're headquartered right there in your sector. It seems that they are using a King Jet to transport some very hazardous bio-waste material. Obviously, Timmons, you know how dangerous that can be."

Timmons was getting into the spirit of the thing as he responded, "Oh, yes sir. Nothing worse than bio-waste."

I continued, "Timmons, we have been tipped off that tomorrow morning at approximately nine o'clock, Lone Star Aviation will be transporting another shipment of bio-waste with their King Jet. We need you to keep that plane on the ground and find the bio-waste. It's very important that you hold everyone in place and keep the jet there until the bio-waste team and the Director arrive from Washington."

Timmons was beside himself. "Do you mean the Director of the EPA, himself, is coming here to Amarillo?"

I adopted a conspiratorial tone and said, "Timmons, that's between you and me, but there's going to be a lot of national media on this, and you know how the Director is. He should be arriving shortly after noon, your time. We will alert all the media from our end, and I know the Director will want you to be available for interviews and a photo session with him."

Timmons interrupted, "That's great. I'll wear my new blue suit."

I continued, "The suit sounds fine, Timmons, but here's the critical thing. You have got to be out there and in place before 9 a.m. tomorrow, and hold that plane until noon. And the last thing is, Timmons, this is between you, me, and the Director. This can't get out to anyone. If this leaked out, Lone Star would dump the material, and the Director would look bad in front of the media. I don't have to tell you what that means for you or me do I, Timmons?"

"No, sir. Hush is the word," Timmons responded solemnly.

I ended the call with, "Timmons, I look forward to meeting you tomorrow. I will be arriving with the Director. I'm glad we can count on you. It's hard to imagine what this is going to do for your career."

I was hanging up the phone as I heard Timmons ask, "What was your name?"

Next, I dialed the Federal Aviation Administration's regional office in Amarillo. I got hold of Buford Caldwell, a genuine good old boy if I ever heard one. He answered the phone by saying, "This here is Buford Caldwell. Can I help you?"

I responded, "Yes, sir. This is correspondent Daniel Edwards with the World News Network. How do you spell Caldwell? I've got to get that right in the story, you know."

He responded cautiously, "C-a-l-d-w-e-l-l. What story?"

I shot back, "You know, your Lone Star Aviation story. We're all over this thing here in Washington. And you can't kid me, Caldwell. I know the regional office has got to be in on this, along with the boys in Washington."

Caldwell sounded baffled as he said, "Listen, Ed. I don't know what you're talkin' about."

I chuckled and responded, "Caldwell, I have to hand it to you. You're a lot sharper than the boys at FAA Headquarters here in Washington told me you would be. They spilled their guts on the story, and you are playing it tight-to-the-vest. I like that, Caldwell. Well, let's leave it this way, then. You didn't tell me anything, but tomorrow at noon, when you impound Lone Star's King Jet and arrest everyone in front of the media, all I'm asking for is a brief, exclusive interview with you that we can get on the international satellites before 1 p.m."

"Say what?" Buford sputtered.

I responded, "Caldwell, I really want to commend you. Sometimes those of us in the international media get a little skeptical in dealing with bureaucrats. But when we meet someone like you that's right on top of this Lone Star situation but smart enough not to tip their hand to the media, it really restores our faith in the system. Sir, it's been a privilege to talk with you. I know you'll be busy at the Lone Star hangar tomorrow right at noon, but afterward, I want to do that exclusive interview and then, sir, it would be a privilege to shake your hand and buy a drink for a true American like you."

I could visualize the tear in Buford Caldwell's eye as he said, "Thank you, sir. It's a privilege to serve."

I hung up the phone and called the Amarillo office of the Drug Enforcement Agency. The phone was answered by a no-nonsense woman who said, "Drug Enforcement Agency. Betty Stevens. May I help you?"

I said, "Miss Stevens?"

She interrupted coldly, "That's *Ms.* Stevens."

I immediately adjusted my game plan and thanked the powers-that-be. I responded, "Yes, ma'am. Ms. Stevens, I'm with the Federal Prisoner Transport Service, and I need to talk to the head man about the prisoner transport tomorrow."

I would have thought it impossible, but her tone got even more frigid. "*I* am in charge here, thank you very much."

"Oh, yes, ma'am, I didn't expect—well—you know."

I paused for a moment and then continued, "Well, sir—or ma'am—if you could just give me an idea of how many prisoners you wanted to be transporting from Lone Star's King

Jet hangar tomorrow at noon, I can have the personnel and vehicles ready."

She shot back, "What are you talking about?"

I responded, "You know, the big drug bust tomorrow at the Amarillo Airport. All the federal agencies are in the middle of this, and I thought since you are right there, you would be directing the entire operation; but maybe they're going to send some men down from one of the district offices or Washington."

Wonder of wonders. Her tone reached a new extreme of frigidity. "Listen to me. I am the duly authorized head of this office, and you can bet if there's going to be a major drug bust at Lone Star's King Jet hangar at noon tomorrow, I will be directing it, not some Johnny-come-lately-pig they send from out-of-town."

I managed to sound respectful and intimidated. "Yes, ma'am, that's why I called you first. We'll just have all of the personnel and transports available on the site at noon tomorrow and wait for your orders."

We hung up.

Next, I dialed the regional office of the Federal Department of Immigration. I got hold of an elderly man named Special Agent Evergreen who had a sinus condition.

I said, "Evergreen, I'm calling on behalf of the Enforcement Division of the Special Prosecutor's Task Force. We need to know if you are going to nail Max and Jim Ed Leland on transporting illegals tomorrow or just let the DEA get 'em on the drug charges."

Evergreen said, "I don't know what you're talking about."

I sounded like a bureaucrat who had solved yet another paperwork problem. "Well, that's what I thought. We'll just let the DEA people have them on the drug charges. There are going to be so many people at Lone Star's King Jet hangar at noon tomorrow, and Betty Stevens at DEA told us that she would take priority over you. We just wanted to check it."

Evergreen displayed admirable backbone as he blew his nose and stated emphatically, "DEA and Betty Stevens do not take priority over us, and you can be assured we will be on the scene."

I ended the call with, "Evergreen, I'm glad to hear that—especially after some of the things that she has said about you in her reports."

Next, I called the Amarillo sheriff's office and the chief of police. I told them I was with the Dallas office of the Associated Press, and asked if they had any comment on the arrests that were going to be made in the Leland matter at noon tomorrow at Lone Star Aviation's King Jet hangar.

They both gave an official-sounding *No comment at this time. Try us tomorrow.* I knew that Amarillo's finest would not let me down.

Finally, I called Bob Arnold, my friend in the federal prosecutor's office in Oklahoma City. I greeted him pleasantly. "Hello, Bob. This is Jacob Dyer. What have you been up to?"

He fired back, "Not much compared to you, Jake. I've seen so much computer traffic and paperwork created on this thing of yours in Amarillo, it sounds like World War III down there. I told you to stay out of this, but I knew you wouldn't; so I warned you that unless you had the Lelands dead-to-rights that there was nothing I could do to help you."

I managed to sound perplexed. "Bob, I don't know what you're talking about. I was just calling to find out if you ever get to Amarillo. You know, Monica and Franklin and I found a neat lake west of town where we had a picnic the other evening. After you warned me about the Leland situation, I decided to drop the whole matter and stay over here in Amarillo for another picnic; and we thought you might want to join us. If you could be at the Amarillo Airport sometime late tomorrow morning, I can have Franklin pick you up."

Bob kept his voice neutral and said, "Jake, you've got your neck stuck out about a mile on this thing."

I sounded unconcerned as I responded, "Well, I know the forecast said it might rain, but it's just a picnic. So, if it rains, we'll eat inside. It's no big deal, Bob."

After a long pause, I heard Bob chuckle. "Jake, off the record, I hope you pull this off."

I responded, "Off the record, Bob, I need you to make sure the Lelands go away, and Becky Ivers is left untouched with Lone Star Aviation intact for her."

"That'll be like removing cancer from a healthy organ, but if you've got absolute proof on the Lelands, I'll do everything I can for Becky," Bob replied.

"Bob, that's all I can ask."

We both hung up, and I sat back to mentally review my handiwork.

I have found over the years that if you want to find dependability within the human species, you've got to rely on traits of pride, greed, and human frailty. They rarely let you down. I still believe in the highest ideals that can be achieved by us humans, but they are rare, indeed. So rare that when you find someone that you can depend on, you've got to make sure that they can depend on you, even if it takes 25 years to repay their loyalty.

CHAPTER 26

ohn Ivers and Becky Owens were to be married the next day. I had been given the honor of serving as best man, and John and I were comfortably settled into our favorite booth at a downtown Tulsa tavern.

I said, "John, as the best man, shouldn't I have planned a bachelor party or something more elaborate than you and me sitting here drinking beer?"

"Well, Okie, there's no place I'd rather be tonight and no one I'd rather be with. We've come a long way, and we've managed to survive through it all."

I offered a toast to John and Becky's health and happiness. John and I touched glasses. We let the silence stretch out between us as only great friends who have shared triumph and tragedy can do.

Finally, I said, "John, I've got to thank you for everything you've done for me. I wouldn't be here without you. You saved my life. You stayed with me through the days on the hospital ship and in rehab. You've helped me discover a new life here in Tulsa and start our new business."

"Your business," John corrected.

"It'll always seem like our business, and I don't know how in the world I'm going to make it without you," I said.

John replied, "Well, Okie, when you finally figure it out, you'll know that this whole lost and found business has been you carrying me. What this kind of deal requires is somebody with brains like you and the ability to get people to do what you want. Somehow, old buddy, you've got this way about you that makes the whole world do what you say. It's like taking candy from a baby."

"I sure don't feel like that," I replied with frustration.

After a brief pause, John replied, "I told you I wouldn't leave you high and dry. And like I said, maybe we can have our cake and eat it, too. I don't think you realize that you've been there for me as much as I've been there for you. I wasn't sure I was going to make it, but I knew that if you could be strong through the blindness thing, the least I could do was not give up on myself and the commitment I made to you.

"So, here we sit, and tomorrow Becky and I will be married, and I'll be flying again—but this time for Lone Star Aviation. And you'll be running your own lost and found agency here in Tulsa. But I think we both still need each other. So, here's the deal. We'll each settle into our new lives, knowing that the other is just a phone call away. Once you feel comfortable on your own, we'll have our own ceremony. Sort of an Independence Day for Jake and John."

"What kind of ceremony do you have in mind?" I asked.

John thought for a minute and replied, "Well, Okie, once you've decided that you're whole again, we'll have a little ceremony to honor who we used to be, who we've become, and all of the friends we lost along the way. You call me when you're ready, and I'll pick you up and fly us both to Washington, DC. We'll stand in front of the Vietnam Wall and drink a toast to better days and the best people."

I replied with more confidence than I felt, "John, you've got a deal."

We touched glasses and drained our beer.

#. #. #.

The Armadillo Lodge has a surprisingly nice pool that we lounged around through the late afternoon and into the evening. We dressed for dinner and went back to Aunt Molly's Kitchen for what we all felt would probably be one of our last meals in Amarillo—win, lose, or draw. We knew that whatever was going to take place would happen like an explosion the next morning.

During dinner, Monica, Franklin, and I violated all laws of civil dinner conversation as we debated religion, sex, *and* politics. We concluded our meal with coffee and a wonderful cherry cobbler that we were assured Aunt Molly had made herself.

Back at the motel, Franklin retired for the evening, and Monica and I went for a walk. I lit a wonderful hand-rolled cigar from the Canary Islands, and I enjoyed the evening and the company.

There are few places I feel comfortable outside of my apartment and my 14th floor corner office in the Derrick

Building. The exception is anywhere I am with Monica. She has a casual way of holding my hand or arm and guiding me through any situation without robbing me of the dignity I need to do my job and feel good about myself.

As we walked up the stairs to our rooms, Monica said, "Well, boss, it looks like you've lit the fuse. All we've got to do now is wait for the explosion."

"I hope it's that simple," I replied. "One of the things John Ivers and I learned in Vietnam is that an explosion can do a lot of strange things. It can hurt people that weren't intended to be hurt, and it can surely blow up the one who lit the fuse."

Monica and I said goodnight and went into our rooms.

I lay back on my bed and, once again, mentally rechecked all of our plans. Once I was satisfied that there was nothing else to do—or if there was, I wasn't aware of it—I picked up the phone and called Becky Ivers at her home on the outskirts of Amarillo. After she said "Hello," I said, "Becky, this is Jake Dyer."

She seemed excited. "Jake, how are you? I haven't heard from you since I left Tulsa. What have you been up to?"

I replied, "Oh, we've been here in Amarillo trying to stir up the hornet's nest and light a few fires under the right people."

"Well, how's it going, Jake?" she asked.

I said, "That's a really long story, Becky, but if you want to watch the final act, we'll pick you up in the morning."

She asked with anticipation, "What's going on, Jake?"

I replied, "Becky, if everything goes well, you'll know soon enough; and if it doesn't, I would just as soon you never knew."

She said with concern in her voice, "Jake, I hope I haven't gotten you into trouble. This really isn't your problem."

I thought for a minute and said, "Becky, 25 years ago, this became my problem, and I want you to know that whatever happens, I've done my best. I just hope it's good enough."

She said, "Jake, I know you've done your best, and John always told me that your best was the best there was anywhere. He told me if I ever got in trouble that all I needed to do was make one phone call to Jacob Dyer."

"He was right," I agreed.

Becky said, "I really never have totally understood this thing between you and John."

I replied, "Becky, when this is all over, I hope I can explain it to you and lay it to rest."

I made arrangements to pick her up in the morning. We both said *goodnight* and hung up the phone.

I lay back on my bed and tried to let sleep take me, but it was slow in coming. I thought of everything I had lost and found again. I hoped that I would be able to keep the life I had and not let it slip away.

## CHAPTER 27

The next morning promptly as arranged at eight o'clock, Franklin knocked on my door and greeted me with the first rumble of the day.

He said, "Sir, everything seems to be in readiness. I have located an ideal spot from which we can observe the day's festivities. I have collected Mrs. Ivers as you requested, and she is waiting for us in our sports utility vehicle with Miss Monica. We have packed the video camera, binoculars, and Miss Monica's camera with the telephoto lens. The morning's bagels and coffee have been procured, and I have taken the liberty of playing a rousing rendition of the *1812 Overture* on the stereo."

I chuckled and said, "Franklin, you're going to make somebody a great wife."

He sniffed and, pretending not to have heard my comment, asked, "Shall we depart, sir?"

We took a roundabout route to the Amarillo Airport. Franklin drove through a gap in the security fence and parked alongside the older Lone Star hangar from which he had shot our video tapes.

Monica said, "There seems to be a rather large hole in the fence back there, Franklin."

He emitted a satisfied rumble and replied, "A horrible breech of security, Miss Monica."

We sat back, enjoying our coffee and bagels to the sounds of the *1812 Overture* and waited for the games to begin. At a little before 9 a.m., according to my Braille watch, Franklin emitted a brief sniff and said, "Sir, there seems to be an official-looking vehicle arriving at the King Jet hangar. Through my binoculars, I can make out the insignia of the Environmental Protection Agency on the door. A small, wiry man has left the vehicle and is now pounding on the door of the hangar."

I chuckled and said, "That would be Timmons. I knew he would be prompt."

Franklin continued the play-by-play. "Sir, now two vans from the Environmental Protection Agency are parking in front of the large aircraft doors to the hangar. A number of individuals are getting out wearing what appears to be some type of space suit, sir."

I replied, "That will be your hazardous bio-waste team, I believe."

Franklin rumbled and said, "Very good, sir. The dark Lone Star Aviation van is now parking behind the EPA car, and the two dark-skinned gentlemen are hastily getting out and approaching the officials from the EPA. I don't believe they are exchanging pleasantries, sir."

Over the next several hours, Timmons made me proud and gave me new confidence in the future of our environment. He was diligent, to say the least. Timmons made the two dark-skinned Lone Star pilots move the jet out of the hangar. He directed the EPA vans to park in front of the jet, blocking any potential escape.

With the Lone Star pilots becoming more and more frantic, the space-suited EPA workers began to examine every inch of the King Jet. They even started taking pieces of the jet apart and lining them up on the tarmac.

Monica said, "Well, Jake, it looks like step one of keeping the jet on the ground until noon is in the bag."

Becky Ivers asked, "Is anyone going to tell me what's going on?"

I replied, "Becky, it's just your tax dollars at work."

Monica periodically recorded the scene with her camera and telephoto lens. She commented, "Pictures may come in handy for a trial or the media. At the very least, it'll be a nice addition to my scrapbook. Do you want any video shot here, boss?"

I thought for a minute and said, "I don't think so. Not yet, anyway."

Franklin rumbled and said, "Sir, I do believe that the proverbial pot is beginning to boil. The dark sedan with the two gentlemen who were previously interested in our movements is arriving, and there are two other gentlemen getting out of the back seat."

Monica said, "Hey, handsome, why don't you hand me those binoculars for a second?"

There was a brief pause, then Monica said, "Now entering—

197

Max and Jim Ed Leland. And they don't seem to be in a good mood this morning."

I lowered my window in the back seat and could hear a number of sirens converging from different directions. I said, "Here comes the cavalry."

I lit a cigar with a Brazilian filler I particularly enjoy and allowed the smoke to drift out the open window.

Franklin continued to describe the scene before us. "Sir, officials from the Amarillo Police Department and the sheriff's office have arrived. There is considerable waving of badges and firearms."

Monica laughed and said, "I hope we are out of range here."

Franklin rumbled in amusement and continued with an account of the arrival of what he described as an assertive woman in a Drug Enforcement Agency vehicle.

I said, "Good old Betty Stevens. Now we'll find out who wears the pants here."

Monica said, "I'll put my money on the lady, thank you very much."

Franklin replied, "She does seem to be formidable. I believe, sir, Ms. Stevens has just put a sheriff's deputy out of the game by kicking him in the shin. Now, sir, vehicles from the Immigration and Naturalization Service are arriving along with official cars from the Federal Aviation Administration. It's beginning to look a bit like a law enforcement convention."

I could hear the first faint sounds of a helicopter overhead. Monica said, "Here comes the media. We've got an Eye-In-The-Sky, and a number of cameramen are jockeying for position. It reminds me of a drunken brawl after one of the St. Patrick's Day parades my uncle took me to when I was a kid."

I checked my watch, and it was 20 minutes until noon. If everything could just hold together a little longer, we were going to make it. And then I felt the unmistakable sensation of a gun barrel being pressed behind my right ear.

I heard the voice of Jim Ed Leland hiss, "I figured I'd find you here. I'd had about all of that down there I could take, and as I was slipping away, I noticed you sitting here and had to come by and pay my respects." He chuckled.

I replied with the most serene voice I could muster, "Good morning, Jim Ed. Beautiful day, isn't it? I believe you know Becky Ivers—the rightful owner of Lone Star Aviation before you stole it—and you've met Monica. But I don't believe you've had the privilege of meeting Franklin."

He barked, "Just shut up, and get out of the car! We're all going to walk real nice and slow into the hangar behind us."

As I got out of the car, Jim Ed said, "Anybody tries anything funny, and this pretty photographer lady gets it."

Monica sounded annoyed as she said, "If you touch me again, you'll wish you hadn't."

Jim Ed laughed and said to Monica, "Pretty lady, we'll have to get to know each other better a little later."

Monica took my arm, and we moved into the hangar which housed the old planes that were the remains of the once-glorious Lone Star fleet.

Jim Ed said, "Now, let's all get into that four-engine job straight ahead of us."

We were forced to climb a shaky ladder, and we were roughly shoved onto sacks of cargo in the back of the plane. I could hear Becky Ivers crying quietly.

Franklin said softly, "Don't worry, ma'am. Everything's going to be all right."

199

I could still hear the sirens and the helicopters focused around the King Jet hangar a few hundred yards away. I asked quietly, "Franklin, any suggestions?"

"Not at this time, sir, but I'm certain something will present itself shortly," he replied.

Jim Ed Leland said, "Everybody just shut up! Don't forget, I've got this nice little gun, and I'm not afraid to use it."

I hadn't forgotten the gun nor the fact that I had gotten everyone into this mess. In a few minutes, I heard the voice of Max Leland say, "Sorry, Jim Ed. It took me a few minutes to get out of there, but all those jerks are so worried about each other, they didn't pay much attention to me."

I heard the aircraft door close, and the huge propeller engines rumbled into life. We began moving slowly across the concrete floor of the hangar. In a few seconds, I could feel sunlight on my face through the window, and I knew we were outside on the tarmac. The plane paused, and the engine sound altered slightly.

I said, "You can't expect to get away with this, you know."

Max Leland replied, "Not only do I expect to get away with it, we *will* get away with it. We always have."

I said, "There's nowhere you can take us that they won't follow. You can't hide."

Jim Ed laughed and said, "We found somewhere to get rid of John Ivers, and we'll get rid of you, too. But for right now, you're our insurance policy that will guarantee to get us down into Mexico."

I could hear Becky as she began crying again. Our suspicions that the Lelands had killed John Ivers were confirmed. Hearing it for a certainty was a greater shock than I imagined it would be. I felt myself sinking into despair. I was as helpless as the day I stood on the rail of the hospital ship in the South China Sea. It seemed that events were moving too fast, and I was unable to stop them.

My best efforts at repaying the long-standing debt I owed were falling far too short.

CHAPTER 28

In the moment of crisis, everything is intensified but moves in slow motion. This is a paradox that has always baffled me. The memory becomes indelibly etched in the mind so that the experience can be relived over and over whenever you want to—and many times when you don't.

I could feel the rough canvas of the cargo sack beneath me. The old engines of the four-prop plane rumbled independently. Franklin whispered covertly, "Sir, I do believe that if the opportunity presents itself, we should definitely avoid allowing this plane to take off."

I answered, "That would be nice."

Monica soothed Becky. "Don't worry, Becky. Jake and Franklin do stuff like this all the time."

I couldn't imagine what she was referring to, but I was glad that she was comforting Becky. She seemed to be the most innocent victim in the whole mess.

Jim Ed shouted frantically, "Everybody just shut up back there!"

"Sounds like you're losing it there, Jim Ed," I observed.

"I'll show you," he said, and I felt a tremendous pain in my ribs as Jim Ed obviously kicked me.

Max called out, "Jim Ed, quit horsing around back there and tell the pilot to get this crate in the air *now*."

I heard Jim Ed walking toward the front of the large cargo plane and the cockpit door being thrown open and banged against the bulkhead.

Jim Ed shouted, "Hurry up and fly this plane out of here!"

The commanding voice of Colonel Deke Sawyer replied calmly, "I don't think so."

Jim Ed sounded menacing as he said, "I want this plane moving right now."

I could hear Deke Sawyer walking toward us as he said, "Leland, if you want this plane moved, you move it yourself."

Jim Ed yelled as if losing control. "I've got a gun here, and you won't be the first pilot I've killed!"

Max said more calmly, "Just relax, Jim Ed. I'm sure we can help our pilot here see the light."

Deke Sawyer chuckled and said, "I've been in the dark for a long time, but now I definitely do see the light."

Max said, "There's no honor in being a dead hero."

Sawyer replied confidently, "I used to know a lot about honor, but in the last few years, it's kind of slipped away."

Jim Ed sounded like he was at the end of his rope when he said, "Listen to me, flyboy. If you don't get up there and get this plane moving, you're going to die with honor."

Colonel Deke Sawyer stated with confidence, "I always hoped I would. But now, I'm going to open this door and help these people out of this plane."

I heard the door opening, and the hot air from the sun-baked tarmac rushed in.

Jim Ed said with certainty, "If you take one step more, I'll shoot you where you stand."

The calm and very welcomed voice of Bob Arnold called from the outside of the doorway, "If you do, it'll be the last thing you ever do. Just put the gun down. You're totally surrounded."

Max Leland said, "Listen, I didn't have anything to do with all this. It was Jim Ed that killed John Ivers."

A shot exploded inside the narrow confines of the cargo plane. I heard a groan, and someone fell to the floor.

Max Leland whimpered in shock, "I can't believe you shot me, Jim Ed."

Jim Ed sounded on the edge of sanity. "You had as much to do with planting that bomb in Ivers' plane as I did. He was going to spill the beans on the whole thing. Now I'm getting out of here."

The second shot was almost deafening. I felt—more than heard—another body fall to the floor of the plane.

Max Leland whined, "You killed my brother."

Bob Arnold said as he stepped across the threshold of the door, "He didn't give me any choice."

Monica took my arm, and we made it down the ladder of the plane and stepped onto the tarmac. Franklin spoke calmly to Becky as he helped her down. "It's okay, ma'am. It's all over now."

I felt a hand come to rest on my shoulder as I heard Deke Sawyer say, "Mr. Dyer, I told you that if I found out this deal was rotten, I'd try to do the right thing."

I said, "Deke, I want to thank you. I don't know what we would have done if you hadn't . . ."

He interrupted. "Jake, I did it more for me than I did for you, but I am looking forward to buying you that drink I promised and have you explain this whole deal to me."

Bob Arnold said in his official voice, "Jake, I told you that you had to have solid evidence on the Lelands if I was going to save your sorry hide. Now one of them's dead, and the other may be dying, every federal and local agency I ever heard of is out here, the media's down everybody's throat, and I don't have one shred of evidence. Can you give me one good reason why I shouldn't arrest you right now?"

Timing is everything.

As we stood on the tarmac, and I contemplated the possibility of a prolonged prison sentence, I heard the blessed sound of a King Jet gliding overhead and landing on the runway.

I said, "Bob, here comes your shred of evidence."

To describe the next two hours as chaotic would be a gross understatement. Betty Stevens took charge of the DEA force that unloaded many boxes of pure cocaine from the King Jet that landed and taxied to the Lone Star hangar. As she directed the collecting of evidence like a general organizing a battle, Special Agent Evergreen from the Department of Immigration, took fourteen illegal aliens dressed in white coveralls into custody.

Buford Caldwell from the FAA was a cross between John Wayne and Marshall Dillon. He arrested the pilot and co-pilot of the newly-arrived King Jet as well as the pilot and co-pilot who had been unable to move the King Jet away from the hangar that morning. Buford's assistants were directed to take a multitude of photographs of the two identical King Jets sitting in front of the Lone Star hangar. Close-up shots were taken of the tail sections displaying the same FAA registration numbers.

As he was directing the removal of his prisoners, Buford Caldwell was actually overheard saying, "You boys are in a heap o' trouble."

The Amarillo police chief and the sheriff were both extremely vocal as they tried to take charge of the entire operation. The media had a million questions, and I feel confident that the hangar at Lone Star Aviation with the two identical King Jets parked outside became the most filmed and photographed scene in Amarillo, Texas history.

By mid-afternoon, everything was beginning to calm down as prisoners and evidence were sorted out and removed by the respective federal and local law enforcement agencies. The media frenzy was subsiding as national and local TV, radio, and newspaper reporters rushed to meet deadlines.

Bob Arnold put his arm around my shoulder as he said, "Jake, when you say you've got evidence, you've definitely got evidence. But what I want to know is, how were you sure that there were two planes?"

I responded guardedly, "Well, we had monitored the King Jet and the hangar enough to know that they were bringing back people and cargo that they didn't take with them, and we confirmed that nothing was picked up in Harlingen. Then when the plane got scratched and dented but came back perfect, there simply wasn't any other explanation."

Bob said, "I don't think I want to know any more. There's

207

just one problem we have here. I've got this little guy from the EPA who can't find any bio-waste."

I laughed and said, "I don't know much about bio-waste, but somehow I think Max and Jim Ed Leland would qualify."

Bob said, "Jake, I'm sorry I couldn't help you out sooner on this deal. Is there anything I can do for you now?"

I thought for a minute and replied, "Two things, Bob. First, there's an air traffic controller named Billy Spears down in Harlingen who needs to get his job back. He was fired for seeing two planes that were really there."

"Sounds easy enough," Bob said.

I responded, "You may have to get him some help with a drinking problem, but I think it'll come under a job-related medical treatment."

"I'll handle it, Jake," Bob assured me.

After a brief silence, Bob asked cautiously, "And the second thing?"

I said, "I told you from the beginning I wanted the Lelands gone and Lone Star Aviation restored to Becky with a clean slate."

"That's not going to be easy, Jake," Bob replied.

I laughed and shot back, "That's why I asked you to handle it, Bob. If it was easy, anyone could do it."

Bob left to organize the final stages of cleaning up the crime scene. I heard a rumble, and Franklin said, "Excuse me, sir, but things do seem to be winding down a bit here, and the ladies are getting rather warm standing on the concrete as they are. And Miss Monica did mention that we missed lunch due to that unfortunate business earlier. Shall I bring our sports utility vehicle around, sir?"

I laughed and replied, "Yes, see to it, Franklin."

As Franklin helped Becky into the front seat of the vehicle and opened the door so that Monica and I could get into the back, I realized—for the first time—that all was right with the world. I couldn't fully understand the weight that had been lifted from my shoulders or the feeling of relief I experienced until I realized that somewhere in the universe where such things are accounted for, a large and long-standing debt had finally been paid in full.

## CHAPTER 29

t was less than two weeks after everything wrapped up in Amarillo. Monica, Franklin, and I were back in Tulsa and settling into our old routine. I was sitting at my desk in my 14th-floor sanctuary of the Derrick building observing my morning coffee and cigar ritual and listening to Aaron Copeland when Princess Monica made her entrance.

She called out, "Good morning, Jake. I've got the bagels, and I want you to know that I am attired in a new gray silk suit—stunning while still professional."

Monica perched on the edge of my desk and spoke more as a friend than an associate. "Jake, I know that you and Becky Ivers are flying up to Washington, DC, today to visit the Vietnam Wall. I don't know what it's all about—and I don't need to know. I just thought you might want a friend to go along."

My thoughts were far away as I heard myself reply absently, "That would be nice."

"That's good, because I already threw a few things into a bag, and Franklin will be here at one to take us to the airport. Becky is picking us up in the King Jet at around one-thirty."

I tried to stay busy throughout the morning, but I knew that my mind was light-years away. Monica startled me back from a distant memory as she said softly, "Jake, we need to go now."

She took my arm, and I carried her bag as we walked out of the office, rode down the elevator, and met Franklin outside the revolving door of the Derrick Building.

We were greeted with a welcoming rumble. "Good afternoon, sir. May I stow the lady's bag?"

Franklin opened the rear door and helped Monica in. As he took her bag, he said, "Sir, I thought since there may be some unanticipated details I could attend to, it might be prudent if I accompanied you to the Capitol this afternoon."

My mind was in a fog as I replied, "That will be fine, Franklin."

He responded with a pleased rumble and said, "Very well, sir. I took the liberty of coming prepared."

The Rolls Royce slid away from the curb and melted into traffic. Before I knew it, we were at the private jet hangar at the Tulsa International Airport. Franklin was just getting the bags out of the trunk as I heard the King Jet taxiing toward us.

Franklin said, "I believe this would be our transportation, sir."

Monica took my arm, and we walked to the boarding stairs. As Franklin loaded our bags, Monica and I sank into the leather upholstery of the palatial jet. Franklin joined us aboard and closed and secured the door.

Becky Ivers kissed my cheek and said, "Jake, thanks for letting me go with you on this special mission."

I replied, "Thanks for going with me and for giving us a ride."

Becky laughed as she said, "I believe you know our pilot."

I heard the unmistakable voice of Colonel Deke Sawyer say, "Good afternoon, sir. A pleasure to serve you today. We'll be flying at an altitude of 41,000 feet. Clear skies and a smooth flight are expected."

I shook hands with Deke Sawyer, and before I knew it, we were cruising high above the earth.

Thoughts of John Ivers dominated my mind. Although I felt my debt had been paid, I had one last task to perform to seal the deal.

We had a smooth landing at Reagan National Airport. At the private jet hangar there was a limousine waiting for us. Franklin transferred the bags from the jet to the car and helped us all into the back.

I overheard him tell the chauffeur who had driven the limo to the airport, "That will be all, sir."

Then a flustered voice said, "And what am I supposed to do?"

Franklin emitted an annoyed sniff and said, "My good man, be so kind as to watch that jet for us."

Franklin navigated through DC traffic, and in a few moments Becky squeezed my hand and said, "We're here at the Wall, Jake."

As Franklin opened the door, Monica asked, "Jake, should Franklin and I wait here or join you and Becky?"

I thought for a moment and replied, "I think John would want all of us there."

Monica took my arm as Becky held my other arm, and we slowly walked to the Vietnam Veterans Memorial. We stood in silence for several minutes, and then I began to speak without being sure who I was talking to.

"John Ivers was a good man and a great friend. He made a promise 25 years ago that he kept until the day he died. On several occasions, he proved to me that his honor was more valuable to him than his life."

I felt myself shift as I began speaking directly to John.

"Well, old buddy, it's Okie here—just like I promised. And I told you whenever I thought I could go it alone, we would come here, drink a toast to one another, and lay our burdens down. I'll never forget you."

At that point, Franklin produced a bottle of champagne from the limousine and poured each of us a glass. We held our glasses, and I announced, "Here is to the good days and the very best people."

As we touched glasses and sipped champagne, I felt whole for maybe the first time in my life. Becky and I reminisced a while, and Monica helped me find the names I knew so well which were carved into the wall.

Finally, something in my soul let me know that it was enough, and I said, "Franklin, it's time to go."

He replied with all the dignity he possessed, "Very good, sir."

Monica took my arm, and Becky resumed her place on my other arm. She was weeping softly as we got into the car.

We were silent for several moments until Franklin cleared his throat and asked softly, "To the jet, sir?"

I couldn't think, but I heard Monica respond, "Yes, Franklin."

Later on the jet, Becky held my hand and said, "Jake, thanks for giving John back his honor and giving me back Lone Star Aviation. I feel like—because of you—John and my daddy can rest in peace."

I asked, "Are you and Lone Star going to be okay?"

She said, "Yes. Deke has helped me decide how to get the fleet back into shape, and we got a great contract carrying medical supply cargo to villages in South and Central America. Not only does the contract mean we're going to be solvent again, it makes me feel like we're doing the right thing."

Deke Sawyer's landing at Tulsa International Airport was so smooth I could hardly tell when we touched the runway. Franklin, Monica, and I climbed down the stairs and stood on the tarmac. Becky and Deke Sawyer joined us for a brief farewell. They got back on the plane, and we stood there until the King Jet rumbled onto the runway and thundered into the sky.

Monica took my arm as we walked to the Rolls Royce limo. Franklin opened the rear door and helped her in. As he held the door for me, he questioned, "Home via the peach orchard, sir?"

I replied, "Yes, indeed, Franklin."

He hesitated, emitted a brief rumble, and said, "Sir, as we are celebrating, I have taken the liberty of selecting an appropriate champagne, and you will find the humidor stocked with some of the forbidden fruit."

As Franklin began to drive us out of the airport complex, Monica asked, "I know what the champagne is, but what—pray tell—is the forbidden fruit?

I chuckled. Through some mysterious means I have never been able to discover, Franklin is able to obtain a fairly steady supply of Cuban cigars.

Monica feigned shock as she said, "Why, Jacob Dyer, those are illegal. How can you—in good conscience—support a Communist regime?"

I replied indignantly as I lit a cigar, "Your majesty, I don't think of it as supporting a regime. It's more like burning their crops."

As I felt the pavement change, I knew that Franklin had pulled off the highway, and we were driving through the peach orchard. I pushed the button on the panel which opened the oversized sunroof, and the wonderful aroma of the peach orchard drifted into the car.

Monica said, "Boss, have I ever mentioned to you that on an average day, you're pretty wonderful? And on a good day, you're a whole lot better?"

I laughed and said, "Your highness, I'm just trying to measure up to the company I keep."

She handed me a glass of champagne and said, "Here's to tomorrow. For the best is yet to come."

We touched glasses.

Far too soon, I realized we were entering downtown Tulsa. My Braille watch told me it was almost midnight.

Franklin asked, "Drop you off at your apartment, sir?"

I said, "No, I believe I'd like to walk home from the office, thank you, Franklin."

As the Rolls Royce stopped at the Derrick Building, Monica touched my hand and asked, "You want some company walking home, Jake?"

"Not tonight," I said.

I unfolded my white cane and stood on the sidewalk until I heard the Rolls Royce slip away. I began strolling down the sidewalk toward my apartment thinking of friends loved, commitments made, and time gone by.

As I crossed one of the empty streets, I felt a fresh breeze blowing from out of the north. For those of us who live in the Southwest, the first cool breeze of fall is like the end of a long winter to those who live in the north.

As I heard the tapping of my cane echo off the buildings around me, I thought about John Ivers and everything he had meant to me. I wondered if I would ever truly believe he was gone—but is anyone ever really gone who makes a difference in someone else's life?

I heard the unmistakable honking of geese flying above me, heading south for the winter. Sometimes I think that they are smarter than we are.

I rounded the last corner and walked toward my apartment building. The odyssey that had begun over a quarter century ago had ended. Or maybe it had just started a new chapter. I didn't know for sure, but for the first time in many years, I was truly excited about tomorrow and what it would bring.

ABOUT THE AUTHOR

Jim Stovall is the author of twelve previous books including the best-seller *The Ultimate Gift* which is now a major motion picture from 20th Century Fox, starring James Garner, Brian Dennehy, and Abigail Breslin.

He is among the most sought-after motivational and platform speakers anywhere. Despite failing eyesight and eventual blindness, Jim Stovall has been a national champion Olympic weightlifter, a successful investment broker, and an entrepreneur. He is the cofounder and president of the Narrative Television Network, which makes movies and television accessible for America's 13 million blind and visually impaired people and their families. NTN's program guide and samples of its broadcast and cable network programming are available at www.NarrativeTV.com.

The Narrative Television Network has received an Emmy Award and an International Film and Video Award among its many industry honors.

Jim Stovall joined the ranks of Walt Disney, Orson Welles, and four U.S. presidents when he was selected as one of the Ten Outstanding Young Americans by the U.S. Junior Chamber of Commerce. He has appeared on *Good Morning America* and CNN, and has been featured in *Reader's Digest*, *TV Guide*, and *Time* magazine. The President's Committee on Equal Opportunity selected Jim Stovall as the Entrepreneur of the Year. In June 2000, Jim Stovall joined President Jimmy Carter, Nancy Reagan, and Mother Teresa when he received the International Humanitarian Award.

Jim Stovall can be reached at 918-627-1000.